D1784714

TALES OF WYCHWOOD

a novel

by Daniel Martin Eckhart

dedicated to Nick, Milo and Ellie

Cover art by Velis Keto

Special thanks to Lady Tania Rotherwick for a walk to remember and for graciously opening up Wychwood to a perfect stranger; to Jim Brannan for taking me into the depths of the forest and for sharing his insights and stories; and to Andrew Compton for welcoming me in Finstock and for giving me the feeling that, through him, I was always there.

This is a work of fiction. While the novel is set in present times and the forest of Wychwood is very real, I have taken certain minor liberties with locations, flora and fauna. As an example, there are no boars in Wychwood – but I simply like the idea of them roaming the forest and so, in Tales of Wychwood, they get to be there. I hope you don't mind.

THE MANY TALES
OF WYCHWOOD FOREST

There have been many special places in the world. Places rich with history and legend, blood and life, love and death. Of all of those many places, no place was more special than Wychwood Forest.

Once upon a time, the forest had spanned England from coast to coast, a vast and magnificent ocean of trees named Arn.

In modern times, it was nothing more than a green dot on a map. Most of the ancient forest had disappeared as humanity had populated the land and claimed it for its many endeavors.

As the forest waned, the tales grew – tales of ghosts and beasts, of witches and goblins and of loved ones, lost to the forest.

From Ascott-under-Wychwood to Leafield and from Ramsden to Charlbury, the stories were told again and again and new ones were added with every strange occurrence.

A sudden death, a vanished dog, a peculiar mist hanging over the fields between Leafield and the forest – the villagers spun them into fresh cautionary tales. Every story was a warning sign – a sign that said "Stay away from Wychwood Forest".

Nowhere were the stories more vivid than in Finstock, the village closest to Wychwood.

In Finstock, more than anywhere else, the forest marked and defined the villagers. As much as they feared the darkness of the forest, they also respected it. Wychwood, with its many tales, was their living history – it was the stories of their ancestors.

The forest was the private property of Lord Francis Thornton. Once a Royal Forest, it had eventually been proclaimed a wildlife preserve. The villagers knew to stay out of the forest ... for unsuspecting outsiders Lord Thornton had surrounded the forest with a tall fence and signs at regular intervals, proclaiming:

No Trespassing!
Wildlife Preserve
(Property of Oakham Park Estate)

Wychwood lay nestled into the picturesque countryside north of Oxford, crouched behind tall hedges and rolling hills – hiding its presence and its stories from the world. Still, occasionally strangers would drive along the road that followed the southern edge of the forest. Even in those briefest of moments, those people would feel what the villagers called "the pull".

Luckily in modern times cars were fast and people would be on their way before the forest was able to get a hold of them. Because if they were to linger for just a little longer, they would stop, they would leave their cars, they would step closer and they would stare, as if hypnotized, into the darkness of the looming trees. They would feel the urge to climb the fence and enter the forest ... and some would disappear forever.

One more thing – Wychwood is a real place.

Should you consider visiting it, be warned.

If you see it, it sees you.

You will likely feel a tingle snaking down your spine. And you will likely dream, for months to come, of walking into darkest green, of gnarly branches reaching for you, of unseen horrors in the darkness, staring, gnashing – just waiting to pounce.

The dreams will pass, although, as one old woman of Finstock was overheard saying one evening at the local pub, The Plough: "Some people never wake from those dreams."

CHAPTER ONE

A CALL
ACROSS THE POND

Roberta Kibble was seventy-six years old when she made the phone call that set it all in motion. She was quite aware that she would gravely endanger the lives of her grandchildren. But if they were anything like their grandmother, they would learn fast and fierce. As a young woman, Roberta's nickname had been "Hatchet" and she had worn that name with pride. She had hacked, she had battled and yes, she had killed. Roberta Kibble wasn't your average grandmother and it very much had to do with the fact that her life, and that of her ancestors, had always been closely connected with Wychwood.

The old woman sat, quite comfortably, in a creaky wicker chair on the patio behind her house in Finstock. Hers was a most unique property, the only house in all of Finstock that was built up against the edge of the forest. All other houses were on the opposite side of Witney Road, at a safe distance from Wychwood. Roberta's house was both typical and unusual.

It was a long building with a thatched roof, originally built in seventeen hundred and ninety-three, added to and fixed up many times since then. The entire property was hidden from the road by a tall hedge. Upon entering the drive way, one instantly felt transported into a different world. The house, quaint in many ways, was surrounded by what seemed like a garden gone wild. Only on second glance did it become apparent that there was method to the apparent wilderness. The flowerbeds, the bushes, the vegetable patches and potted plants were all carefully tended and the walkways between them made every plant easily accessible.

The rectangular piece of land was flanked on three sides by the forest. Aside from the house and the sprawling garden, the property contained three large old beech trees, a dozen boulders with swirling lines carved into them and a rickety shed near the edge of Wychwood.

Roberta Kibble took a sip from her lemonade and smiled a grim smile. She looked at the phone on the table next to her. An old phone, rotary, with a long cord that snaked back into the house. She scratched her unruly white hair. Wild woman. Witch. Nobody called her witch to her face, but Roberta knew that it was what they called her in the village. She didn't mind as it wasn't meant in any sort of mean-spirited way. Quite the opposite. The villagers treated her with reverence … and they came, often late at night, when they needed a remedy. Roberta's garden was well known as it seemed to contain just about any herb anyone had ever heard of. And the concoctions of the Witch of Wychwood often helped.

They're telling stories about me, Roberta thought and chuckled. She had long ago become the protagonist in many of the tales of Wychwood. The villagers had no idea of half the stories, the stories told only within the forest. The chuckle became a cough and the cough became so violent that Roberta curled into a knotted ball.

"Meow," the calico cat said, rubbing its head against the leg of the old woman.

Roberta, breathing heavily, opened her eyes, her face close to the cat. She winked at it, then pushed herself back into an upright position. She collected and tasted the bile in her mouth. The taste of death, she reflected calmly. Roberta took a deep breath and then spit the phlegm, with perfect accuracy, into an empty flower pot just beyond the patio.

"Corisander," Roberta said while scratching her nose, "You wouldn't mind a few additional house guests, would you?"

The cat looked from her to the forest and back. Corisander had appeared at her house three years ago and the name "Corisander" had popped into Roberta Kibble's head and that had been that. Roberta had soon realized that Corisander was different in many ways. Different was good and Roberta appreciated the company. Corisander was there when needed, to listen, to warn, to give comfort. And he most definitely understood the dangers of the forest.

"I'll be here to protect them," Roberta said.

"Meow," the cat replied and curled up in the old woman's lap.

"Oh, shut up," she muttered, gently scratching the cat

just below the chin. "I'll test them and I'll train them. They are my only chance to get Chester back," she added grimly. "Well then, let's call the other side of the big pond."

She picked up the receiver and dialed a long number. The cat watched the rotary dial as it was pulled one way with every new number, then rattled back into its original place. The sound of the phone's dial seemed amplified in the twilight of the evening. And when Roberta listened to the phone ringing across the Atlantic in distant New York City, it seemed as if the forest were listening, too.

"Hello?" a man's voice said and she recognized it instantly even though they hadn't spoken in years. Andrew Murphy was an Irish-American journalist who had met Roberta's only daughter Lily during a visit to Oxford seventeen years ago. Lily had, even then, left Finstock behind, wanting nothing to do with the family business. They had started a family in New York, in a nice place in Brooklyn, and Lily had been adamant from the start that she wanted her children to never visit Finstock. Even during Roberta's one visit to America eight years ago, Lily had impressed on her that she was not to tell the children any stories.

"Hello Andrew, it's Roberta," she loudly called into the phone.

"Roberta? How are you? Is everything okay?"

"How's Lily?" Roberta shouted.

"I'm afraid there's been no change, Roberta."

"I see. And how are the children?" Roberta shouted.

"I can hear you just fine, Roberta. The kids are, oh you

know, kids. All good, I guess. Ellie's still my little princess. She's just turned twelve, going on sixteen."

"Twelve's a good age to begin," Roberta said to herself.

"Begin what?"

"Oh, nothing, nothing. How about the boys?"

"Milo's fourteen and, well, it's a bit difficult to explain, Roberta. Tell me, how are you?" Andrew said, trying to switch topic.

"What's wrong with Milo?"

"Well, he … he's in therapy."

"Therapy? Whatever for?"

"He has these bursts. Gets angry and hits class mates. He's been in three fights this year alone. It's … it's tough. But I'm sure it's just a phase."

"Does he win the fights?" Roberta asked.

"What?"

"The fights, Andrew, does he win the fights?"

"What? Well, in fact, yes, but that's immaterial, Roberta," Andrew said gruffly. "Milo's behavior is highly concerning."

"Yes, of course," Roberta said and smiled. Three fights and won them all. "How about Nick? He's what, sixteen now?"

"Yes. Nick's fine. Well, as far as I know he's fine. He spends most of his time in his room with his computers. Teenagers, right?"

"Right," Roberta said and left a purposeful pause. The time had come.

"Roberta? Are you still there?" Andrew asked.

"… Yes," she said, giving her voice a creak with a pinch of a croak.

"Is there something wrong?"

"Well, you know, old age," Roberta said as she stroked the cat. "And then there's been that diagnosis," she added.

"What diagnosis?" Andrew asked, sounding alarmed.

"It isn't the best of news, I'm afraid. It appears that I have cancer and I'm told that I have no more than a few months left to live."

"I … I'm so sorry, Roberta. So terribly sorry. Is there anything I can do?"

"Yes, there is something, Andrew," Roberta said. "Could you come?"

"Come? Me? I'm not sure that I …"

"No, Andrew. What I meant is, could all of you come? Please. I'll soon be gone from this Earth and I want to see my daughter and my grandchildren one more time. And my son-in-law, too, of course. I'd fly if I could but the doctor says I won't be able to travel anymore."

Andrew was silent. Roberta knew him to be a wonderful man, always on the right side of things. He would never want to act against the wishes of his wife. Lily had been clear, very clear. She had never given Andrew an explanation as to why visiting Finstock was out of the question. Was it bad family history? An issue with her mother? Did something terrible happen during her upbringing there? Andrew didn't know … and Andrew would never need to know. It was better that way.

"I promised Lily, Roberta …"

"I know. I know, Andrew. I understand that this is difficult for you," Roberta said. "But Lily has been ... away for years now. She won't even know she's come here. But I'll know. And the children will know. They will know where her mother's family came from. They will know their roots. It'll be good for them. Please, for just a few weeks. It'll be a summer vacation for them, Andrew. The best vacation of their lives ..."

"Wouldn't it be stressful for you, in your condition ...?"

"It'll be the best medicine, Andrew," Roberta said, full of hope. "There's plenty of room and the beds are already made."

CHAPTER TWO

THE CAT THAT WASN'T

He had been there in the beginning. He remembered the time of the round and the flow, a time when imagination had been truth, a time when colors had been alive and when one had been all. It had been a time long before the continents, long before form had slowed into solid shape. He had been a wind and a shade, a gleam and rustle, a waterfall and a mountain. With the changing of the world he had been forced to choose – and had chosen the shape of the cat.

It was a good shape, better than most. In this shape, he had roamed the lands to discover the remnants of the flow, the places, the creatures, the sparks. Traces resided in the most unusual places as there were no limits to the creativity of the flow. At times a spark would be within a child, at times within a pebble. Human beings had their own names for it. In people, they called it talent, genius, insanity … and sometimes they called it the kiss of the muse. And where some humans felt a tingle, they called those places high energy spots, vortices and ley lines. All it was, however, was remnants of the flow.

Trying to make sense of things had always been humanity's greatest deficiency, something the cat had realized thousands of years ago. They had come, they had multiplied, they had brought the noise and they had conquered the world by the sheer power of their numbers. Ever since that time they were trying to make sense, asking the same questions ... and they would never be content with the answers. Humans. Corisander lightly shrugged his feline shoulders. He had spent lifetimes with the brightest of minds, some of them able to go with the flow, some of them slipping into madness – the simplicity of life too easy for their convoluted minds.

The cat had jumped off Roberta's lap and, sitting in the grass, was watching her. The old woman was dying and the old woman was happy. Happy because five people from another part of the world would travel to be with her. She had hung up the phone, drank from her lemonade and talked to herself, to Corisander, to the forest ... the cat didn't listen.

Corisander couldn't tell the future. No one could and anyone suggesting otherwise was a fool. The future did not exist. The cat knew that Roberta Kibble hadn't been honest. There was a plan, an agenda, a reason behind the reason that would mean mortal danger for three children. The old woman was full of hope, Corisander knew – and maybe everything would turn out exactly as Roberta hoped. But in Corisander's experience deception didn't spin that way. One way or another, lies always brought cracks, scrapes and cuts into the flow.

The cat lay down in the high grass. As always, Roberta only mowed when it became near impossible to push the lawnmower through what any lawn-loving Englishman would have undoubtedly called disgraceful. During Roberta's phone call, there had been no wind, as if the forest had been holding its breath, not a leaf had whispered in the trees. Now a light breeze was picking up and the cool of the night pushed from the forest toward the house.

"Meow," the cat said and Roberta Kibble nodded tiredly. Corisander knew of the cancer that was radiating malevolently within her. The cat would miss the old woman. She sighed heavily as she pushed herself up and out of the chair.

"My only chance," she said again as she placed everything onto a tray. "... and I get to see my Lily again, that's something, isn't it? And my grandchildren, well ... we shall see soon enough. Maybe I shouldn't have called, my friend," she said to the cat. "Maybe I should have just let it all go ... but you know what? At this moment I am happier than I've been in a very long time."

Corisander gave the old woman a light nod and watched as she carried the tray into the house. She returned once more, collected the phone, rolled up the cord and gave the cat a final smile. She would have her night cap, a glass of Irish whiskey, after brushing her teeth and then she'd be asleep within minutes. Her door would be open and Corisander would sneak into her bedroom later tonight and sleep on the chair by the window. Same as every night.

A mouse scurried through the leaves of grass and came to a wide-eyed stop right in front of the cat's nose. Corisander didn't move. The mouse, frozen in terror, just stared. Then it felt a strange calm flood its fragile body and the shivering disappeared. The mouse didn't understand, couldn't understand, and yet it felt that there was nothing to fear from this creature that lay there in the shape of a cat. It lightly twitched for a moment, then darted away. The cat listened to the sounds of the mouse, heard it running, heard it scrape down into a hole. Corisander reached out beyond a cat's hearing and sensed the mouse coming to rest in a little cave. The mouse panted, rolled itself into a ball against the warmth of three other mice and fell asleep confused and exhausted.

For a moment Corisander lost himself in the sounds, the smells and the colors of the forest, all of his senses reaching into the riches beyond the fence. He felt countless shades of colors rolling and merging, growing, expanding. Corisander felt boar and deer, squirrels and hares, foxes and badgers. There was life everywhere, accompanied by the goodnight songs of the birds and the last flutters of the bees and butterflies.

And deep within the forest, in the trees above and the caves beneath, older creatures were roaming.

CHAPTER THREE

THE ARRIVAL
OF THE AMERICANS

It was four days later and Roberta Kibble was ready for the arrival of the Murphy family. Truth be told, she had been ready two days before already. The moment Andrew had called back, confirming their trip with the flight details, Roberta had turned into a whirlwind. The cat had, in wise recognition, left the house and stayed away while Roberta swept every nook and cranny. She changed the linen on all the beds, fluffed the pillows, aired every room. She dusted places she hadn't dusted in decades, including the attic. A dozen very confused and greatly annoyed spiders were forced to vacate the premises. Roberta cleaned the windows, washed the curtains and scoured and polished the kitchen top to bottom.

Images of the coming days kept flowing past her inner eye. She saw herself playing with the children, telling them stories, their own stories, stories they deserved to know about.

Roberta imagined the astonishment in their eyes, the excitement, the pride and all the while she was only too aware that her imagination was just that, imagination. Anything might happen. The children might very well hate the place and it was entirely possible that they would care neither about her nor about their ancestry. Didn't they have their own lives? She really had no right to pull them into her world. Roberta, sitting at the gleaming kitchen table, sunk her head into her hands and felt older than she'd ever felt before. Selfish old woman, she thought.

Another image floated past. The image of her daughter Lily, walking with her mother, hand in hand, laughing, talking, content in each other's company. Wishful thinking, that was. Everything she had ever taught her daughter, Lily had rejected. Roberta had tried to guide her in every conceivable way but with everything that had happened, Lily's choice had not come as a surprise. Leaving Finstock, leaving everything, leaving her mother.

Her illness … Roberta had often wondered about it. During her one visit to the United States, she had seen the beginning of it. Her daughter had begun to forget things, places, names, words. Roberta had prescribed and sent a variety of herbal potions but according to Andrew they didn't help. Neither did any of the many doctors they consulted. Tests had been made and then more tests and over the years Lily had retreated to another place. She had stopped talking, she had stopped smiling and she had completely stopped acknowledging people. Roberta could only imagine what it is was like for Andrew and the children.

No more conversations, no more encouragements, no hugs, no kisses. Lily simply existed and seemed entirely fine where she was. She dressed herself, she ate, she stared, she slept. None of it made sense to anyone … and yet Roberta harbored the unfounded hope that, somehow, coming back to Wychwood might help Lily.

The rattle of a car engine made her jump to her feet, sending the chair crashing to the floor. She hurried to set it back, neatly, then wiped her dress, quickly brushed through her hair and then dropped the brush into a drawer. They were coming. They were here.

When she stepped outside, she did so with perfect calm and a smile on her face that, she figured, was a grandmotherly type smile. She wasn't surprised to see that, even before the car was in sight, the cat was already sitting by the door.

A big white car turned off Witney Road into the drive way and stopped in front of the house. Andrew sat behind the wheel, looking thin and worn. Next to him was Lily, beautiful Lily, staring into space. The backseat was occupied by the three children and they all had their eyes on Roberta. She smiled and, for a moment, received nothing in return. Then Andrew waved as he shut off the engine – and Ellie sent her a timid smile.

Roberta stepped forward as Andrew approached her for a strong handshake and a quick and awkward embrace.

"Hi, Roberta," he said, looking at her with doleful eyes.

"Hi, Andrew," she replied. "It is so wonderful that you have all managed to come."

"Of course," Andrew said, then realized that everyone else was still sitting in the car. He hurried to open the door for Lily and waved at the children. "What are you waiting for? Come say hello to your grandmother!"

Roberta watched intently as her daughter stepped from the car. Lily looked past her, past the house, recognizing nothing, seeing nothing. When Andrew let go of her hand, she took a few steps into the garden and sat down in the grass, her face raised to the clouds. Roberta heard the rear doors open and turned to see the three children standing there. While all of them had their mother's black hair and green eyes, Nick and Ellie were tall and slender while Milo was considerably shorter and stocky.

Then Roberta did something that she most certainly hadn't planned on doing – and most definitely hadn't imagined as a possibility. She had never been the motherly type and knew nothing about being a grandmother, but when she saw the three young faces standing there, it just happened. Her heart swelled and a smile bright as the sun spread across her face. Without a word she stepped forward and pulled all of them into a hug that just may have been one of the best hugs of all times. The awkwardness of the moment melted away from the children and they embraced their barely known grandmother just as intensely.

"Picture moment if ever there was one," Andrew said, snapping a few shots of the group hug with his phone. The spell was instantly broken. Roberta and the children let go of each other and grinned uncomfortably at their shoes, the house, the garden and the trees, anywhere but at each other.

"How you have grown!" Roberta exclaimed, stepping

back from the children. She ruffled Milo's hair and it was obvious that he hated it. Nick cautiously busied himself with the luggage in the back of the car. Roberta smiled. "Don't worry, no more hugging for a bit."

"I didn't mind," Ellie said, looking up at Roberta with a bright smile on her face as she sat down in the grass next to her mother.

"Doesn't look like Mom recognizes any of it," Milo uttered.

"Sometimes things are happening even if we don't see them, Milo," Roberta replied.

"Do you think Mom will come back?" Ellie asked, her eyes clinging to her grandmother.

"Oh, I don't know, Ellie, I don't know," Roberta said, putting an arm around her as they watched Lily lie down in the grass and closing her eyes. "But I do know some things. I know that you have come to a wondrous place. Welcome to Wychwood!"

Roberta's call was swallowed up by the forest. For a moment, they all stood and looked at the dark wall of trees that spread high and deep beyond the property.

"So this is it," Nick said into the silence.

"Yes, this is Wychwood." Roberta proclaimed with a smile and wondered whether they already felt the pull of the forest. Looking at their faces, she couldn't tell. Ellie seemed more focused on her mother. Both Nick and Milo appeared intrigued but nothing more while Andrew was busy carrying their luggage to the door.

"The place Mom never wanted us to visit," Milo added.

"Oh, come on," Andrew interjected, exasperated. "Look around, it's beautiful here. This is where your mother was born, where she grew up!"

"The place she never wanted to come back to," Nick added.

"Stop it. Now," Andrew said gruffly, sending Nick a severe nod that was clearly intended to make him think about his dying grandmother. Roberta decided to take over.

"Well, please do come in," she offered cheerily. "I'll show you your rooms and when you've unpacked, we'll make ourselves comfortable in the garden with Roberta Kibble's Famous Lemonade and freshly baked biscuits."

***

Corisander followed them into the house. Roberta led them upstairs and showed them their bedrooms, one for each of them, all of them with windows facing the forest. The guests followed Roberta and listened as she explained this and that about the rest rooms, the towels and the long history of the house.

"Makes yourselves comfortable," Roberta said brightly. "I'll call as soon as I'm ready downstairs," she added, beamed at them once more, then hurried down the stairs.

Corisander walked from room to room. In one, Lily sat on the bed, staring at the leaf pattern of the room's wallpaper, while Andrew hung some clothes into the wardrobe and placing others into the chest of drawers.

"We're here, Lily. Finstock. Wychwood," Andrew softly announced as he hung one of her flower dresses into the wardrobe. Had he watched her face at that moment, he might have seen just the slightest twitch at the mention of Wychwood. He continued talking as he had done for years, filling the void, talking to himself. He had given up hope a long time ago and yet the monologues continued. Maybe, wherever she was, she could hear him. Maybe, despite everything they had come to know over time, it made a difference.

"Flight was okay, wasn't it? Jetlag and all, we'll sleep like babies tonight. Never thought I'd come back here. Remember the one time you brought me here to meet her? I don't think I've ever been more scared, trying to make a good impression." Andrew turned to Lily, took her face into his hands and gently kissed her. There was no reaction and although she looked right at him, she didn't see him. "I've loved you so much then, Lily. And I love you even more today ... Lily, please come back to me."

As Corisander meandered from room to room, he saw Ellie engrossed in the many pictures framed on the wall opposite her bed. Family pictures. Men, women, children. Standing together, standing alone. Portraits one and all. The cat knew that Ellie was wondering about the fact that everyone in those pictures was armed with everything from bows and arrows to knives and axes.

Passing the next room, the cat saw Nick sitting on the bed, frustrated with his laptop computer. A little side-effect of the forest, it didn't show a particular fondness for modern technology. Corisander arrived at the last room and entered.

Milo stood in front of the open window, immobile, gazing out at the forest's edge. Wychwood, glowing in shades of deepest green, seemed to creep into the rooms. As Corisander approached the boy in absolute silence, Milo turned to acknowledge the cat's presence. He's sensed me coming in, Corisander thought ... interesting. As surprising as it had been to observe Ellie climbing the stairs earlier. The house's staircase was old, the steps mostly the original boards and they creaked their age with pride ... and yet, when Ellie had climbed those stairs, there had been barely a sound, almost as if the child were floating up.

"Hey cat," Milo said and turned to look at the forest again.

Corisander jumped onto the bed and curled up. A light wind moved the curtains and, beyond the windows, the branches of the trees swayed, leaves rustling, whispering, greeting the new arrivals.

Nick came into the room, sitting down next to Corisander. The cat gave a light meow as Nick's hand began to stroke its back. The cat turned onto its back. Corisander liked belly rubs and Nick obliged.

"What?" Milo asked without turning around.

"Nothing," Nick muttered.

"No Wi-Fi?"

"Of course not," Nick sighed, clearly frustrated. "We're lucky Grandma has electricity."

"Feels like someone's looking at me," Milo said out of the blue.

"What are you talking about?" Nick asked.

"I don't know. The forest is … weird," Milo replied.

"Wychwood already getting to you?" Nick suggested, rolling his eyes.

"There are lots of family pictures in my room," Ellie proclaimed, standing in the door frame.

"Can't wait to see them," Nick said flatly, smacked Milo lightly against the back of the head and followed Ellie.

Milo remained, eyes on the forest.

CHAPTER FOUR

THE BLACK BEAST
AND OTHER TALES

It was late afternoon. The land between the house and the forest had long sunk into the shadows of the trees and Roberta served the Murphys tea, lemonade and biscuits. Sitting out there on the patio, they looked at the dark trees beyond the fence and the leaves of the oak and the beech seemed to be dancing.

Nick, Milo and Ellie sat in the chairs, with the cat in Ellie's lap. Lily rested on top of one of the carved stones, knees pulled to her chin. Andrew stood next to her and caressed her cheek once more before joining the others.

"Those stones are beautiful," Ellie said.

"My husband made them, Henry Kibble. He was a stone mason, you know. Best for miles and miles around. The circles and all of those lines … Henry told me once that sometimes he could see the world that way. Everything in flow," she said softly, remembering Henry. Then, snapping back, "So what do you know about Wychwood?"

"The name has nothing to do with witches," Ellie said eagerly. "It comes from the Hwicce, an Anglo-Saxon tribe."

"You're quite right, Ellie," Roberta said. "Although,

there are those who do call your grandmother a witch, you know." For a moment they all looked at her and an owl hooted a single hoot deep within the woods. Roberta winked. "What else do you know?"

"Whatever's on the web," Nick said.

Roberta knew that he meant the internet. Marvelous thing from all she'd heard and perused for herself at the village library computer. But she also knew that none of the truth would be found there. The real truth could only be found within the forest. Nick matter-of-factly relayed the children's research. They knew a surprising amount, Roberta realized and as Nick talked, both Milo and Ellie occasionally added more. Between the three of them, they seemed to know a lot of the forest's history and especially of the many supernatural tales that had traveled beyond the villages over the course of the centuries.

"Do you believe in such things?" Roberta asked them evenly.

"Of course not," Andrew said, smirking. "But everybody loves a good tale, right? When my granddad left Ireland for the US he brought along nothing but the clothes on his body, a button accordion, a love for Irish tales and the talent to tell them. And boy could he tell them, stories about the ancient heroes and kings and queens of Ireland, stories of fairies and giants, banshees and ghosts."

"So you think they're all just fairytales," Roberta said.

"For the most part, sure," Andrew said. "Though some of the fiction was no doubt based on bits and pieces of fact … and some were simple cautionary tales."

"Like Little Red Riding Hood," Ellie said. "It was a story to make sure children would remember to stay on the path. Because the wolves were real."

"Yes, the wolves were real," Roberta echoed.

"What about the Black Beast?" Nick asked.

"Oh, please, Nick," Andrew said, with an apologetic shrug to Roberta. "He loves the idea of some mythical beast roaming free."

"Ah, the Black Beast," Grandma Kibble said with a smile. "Toby Edwards says he saw the black creature and it was big as a house and caused his car to crash into a tree. It later turned out that old Toby had enjoyed a few ales too many that night. Millicent Marstin over in Ramsden says her great grandfather saw the beast as well, the size of a bull, apparently. I do have to add that Henry Marstin was best known as the Ramsden village fool and died believing that he was King of both England and China."

"There goes that story," Andrew said with a satisfied smirk in Nick's direction. "When you guys do your research, you really should check your sources, too. Sure there are black beasts, they're called cats. As for black panthers roaming Oxfordshire, those stories are about as real as the Loch Ness monster, Big Foot and the Yeti. Ever wonder why there's not a single piece of solid evidence on any of those creatures?"

"Maybe there's no evidence because those creatures are experts at hiding," Nick evenly suggested.

"Or they're experts at eating those who discover them," Milo added.

"Fairytales," Andrew said, toasting Milo with his glass of lemonade.

"So why's Wychwood closed?" Nick asked.

"Well, it is a private forest. It's part of Oakham Park Estate and belongs to Lord Francis Thornton. When he was a young man, he decided to turn Wychwood into a wildlife preserve. The fence keeps out hikers and because of that, in there, you'll find rare flora and fauna."

"Have you ever been in there?" Milo asked.

"Of course," Roberta said with a mischievous smile. "I go in all the time … but please don't tell his Lordship."

"Can we go in?" Ellie asked.

"Let's see about that tomorrow," Roberta said.

"Who's ever heard of private forest," Andrew said, his eyes closing for a moment. As he helped himself to another sip of lemonade, so did the children.

"Why is your lemonade green, Grandma?" Ellie asked.

"Why, if it were yellow it'd be regular lemonade and not Roberta Kibble's Famous Lemonade, you see?" she said with a wink.

"There's something strange about the forest," Milo said, doing his best to keep awake.

Roberta nodded as she looked from one to the other. They were all sleepy, both lemonade and biscuits were working their magic. The new arrivals would spend their first night in Finstock sleeping deeply and soundly.

"It's been a long day," Andrew said tiredly as he rose. "Time to hit the sack, kids."

"I'm glad you're here," Roberta said. As she pushed

31

herself out of the chair she managed to ruffle Milo's hair once more before he had a chance to duck away.

"I'm glad, too," Ellie said and gave her grandmother a hug.

"Yeah," Nick added with the hint of a smile in his grandmother's direction. That sign of affection, coming from Nick, was worth two hugs and Roberta knew it. She acknowledged it with a smile and a nod.

"You're home, children," Roberta said as she walked away into the house. "You're home."

Nick, Milo and Ellie looked at each other, looked at their father. Andrew Murphy gave a light shrug and ushered them all into the house. Before he was able to close the kitchen door, the cat snuck in as well.

When Roberta looked in on all of them later on, Nick's door was closed. Lily was asleep and Andrew and Ellie were still talking. They were in the room across the hallway, a long room, the length of the house, part library, part study, part music room. Roberta found the door to Milo's room ajar, darkness inside. She opened the door wide enough for her head to squeeze in. Milo lay in bed, with Corisander curled up at his feet.

"Ah, there he is," Roberta said softly.

"He just came," Milo mentioned drowsily.

"That's Corisander for you."

"Corisander ... weird name."

"Weird is a curious word, dear Milo. And in the case of Corisander I'd say it couldn't be more fitting."

"Is it okay if he stays here?" Milo asked, half-asleep

already.

"Certainly. If he's here, he means to be here."

Roberta was about to leave when a mellow Irish melody softly floated their way. An accordion lightly followed the gentle whistles of a flute.

"Dad and Ellie," Milo mumbled.

"It's beautiful," Roberta said and realized that Milo was asleep. She looked at him for another moment, then her eyes went to the forest beyond the open window. Wychwood was barely visible in the night, hidden in the darkness of an overcast night sky.

Leaning against the wall in the hallway, Roberta listened to the accordion and the flute for another while. They were here, they had returned.

So far, so good, Roberta thought.

CHAPTER FIVE

A WYCHWOOD DREAM

He stood on top of the highest beech tree, below him the forest, stretching to the horizon in every direction. The sky was a crisp blue and the breeze played with his hair. The boy's arms were crossed and his eyes closed. He stood, swaying with the movement of the tree, one with the tree, in perfect balance. When he opened his eyes, a smile played around his lips. He unfolded his arms and spread them wide, like wings.

Milo jumped. For an instant, he seemed suspended in the air, an image of serene calm and peace. As gravity set in, the boy fell.

With the grace of a squirrel he landed on the tree below, barely touched the branch and instantly bounded off to the next tree. Silvery gray forest pigeons rose into the air, startled as Milo rushed past them. He jumped again, added a pirouette as he soared higher, then followed it up with a graceful somersault.

As he continued jumping from tree to tree, squirrels appeared, first one, then two, then a dozen. They gave chase and followed the boy like dolphins, racing a ship's bow. They crisscrossed his path until they reached a clearing, a distance too wide for them to cross. As the squirrels stopped, Milo grinned, leapt and flew.

In flight, he turned and waved back at the chattering squirrels. Milo effortlessly rose above the trees, into the chill of the clouds, then zoomed back into the forest where he landed in a sun-drenched clearing.

A boar looked up, gave an annoyed grunt and attacked. Milo's grin widened as he raced across the clearing, too fast for the tusks behind him. He jumped and was, once more, in the trees.

He laughed out loud when he realized that he was surrounded by the squirrels again. They chattered eagerly and loudly, wanting the chase to go on.

Milo was happy to oblige.

Again he picked up the pace, leapt, bounced and jumped, always one step ahead of the squirrels.

Below him and around him eyes seemed to watch his every move.

The trees moved with him and so did the ground far below, flowing like a dark green river.

***

It was darkest night as Corisander's eyes opened. Milo was climbing out of his bed, stood there, wavering for a moment, then he opened the door and left the room. Curious, the cat followed. The boy stumbled down the stairs and Corisander saw that he was asleep.

The pull, Corisander realized in surprise.

As Milo walked through the kitchen toward the back door, the cat's claws slashed into the boy's foot. Milo gave a low moan but steadily continued. He unlocked the door and stepped out into the night.

When Corisander followed Milo, he felt the pull of the forest more strongly than ever before. As if on strings, the boy was drawn toward Wychwood.

Corisander bit into Milo's ankle. It didn't wake the boy, it didn't stop the boy. He put one foot in front of the other, making his way across the wet grass toward the forest's edge. Hard as Corisander tried, the boy continued on his path. When Milo's feet were bleeding from slash after slash, Corisander charged through the cat flap back into the house.

He reached Roberta's bed and found her already sitting up straight. Seeing Corisander, Roberta rushed to her feet and hurried after him. We may be too late, Corisander thought. When he ran out into the garden again, he saw Milo at the fence, trying to climb it. The cat sped to the boy and cursed humanity and cats alike. Why did he have to choose the shape of a cat? And why did the old woman have to be so slow?

The boy slipped down, then climbed again as Roberta slammed open the kitchen door. She rushed, barefoot and her nightgown flying, toward them.

"No, no, no, no," the old woman exclaimed. She wrenched Milo down, turned him around and as she did, he struggled to turn back to Wychwood.

"Milo," Roberta urged. "Milo, wake up!"

Milo stopped. For a moment he just stood there, eyes lowered, seeing nothing. Then suddenly Milo twisted and slipped from Roberta's fingers. She stepped after him, grabbed him as hard as she could, shook him, shook him again. When nothing seemed to help and Milo was about to twist free again, she slapped him.

Milo woke with a gasp.

"Why are my feet bleeding?" Milo said, staring down, dazed.

Roberta sighed with relief and smiled at the boy as he looked her in confusion. She took him by the shoulder, turned him around and led him to the kitchen door.

"Let me get you a cup of Roberta Kibble's Famous Late Night Tea," she said. As they entered the house, Milo looked back to the forest once more, as if trying to remember something.

"There's something in there," Milo said.

"Yes," Roberta replied. "But everything's quite all right now."

Roberta sat the boy at the table, waited for Corisander to slip into the house, then locked the door and put the key into the pocket of her night robe. Corisander jumped onto the window sill and watched both the forest and the actions of the old woman. As Milo sat there, still half asleep, Roberta put on the kettle, collected leaves from jars and herbs from pouches. As she sliced roots and prepared her brew, she always kept her eyes on the boy.

"Do you remember anything, Milo?"

"I had a dream," he answered.

"What about?" Roberta asked casually. Corisander felt the old woman's tension.

Milo began to remember, the forest, the squirrels, the jumps and the flights. It all came out, little by little, as he sipped from the old woman's tea, as she tended the cat-inflicted wounds. She retrieved a large jar, scooped golden-brown balm from it and spread it across Milo's feet. As she wrapped bandages, the boy remembered more.

"The forest was … alive."

"Alive?" Roberta asked, frowning.

"Yes," the boy replied as a shiver ran through his body.

"It was just a dream," Roberta suggested. "There is no need to be afraid."

"No, it was … beautiful," Milo said to her surprise.

Corisander watched as Roberta made Milo drink a second cup of tea, then a third. Soon he would sleep. A little while later she pulled Milo to his feet. Corisander jumped off the sill and followed. Roberta guided Milo up the stairs and the boy, almost asleep, smiled. When he was in his bed, Roberta tucked him in and Corisander took up his place at Milo's feet again.

"Best not mention the sleepwalking to your dad," Roberta said softly.

"Okay," Milo murmured.

"All right if I close the door?" Roberta asked softly.

"Meow," Corisander replied.

She lightly nodded, smiled and closed the door. In the darkness of the room, Corisander heard the boy's breathing. Sound and deep. The cat listened into the boy and felt only peace. Then the cat listened into the old woman down in the kitchen.

Roberta hadn't gone to bed yet. She was awake, wide awake, as she tidied up the kitchen. Her mind was reeling. She knew the pull of the forest. She had lived with it all her life. But to the best of her knowledge it had never been this strong.

Corisander left the old woman when he knew that she was calm enough to rest. The cat mused about the boy's dream and the pull that he himself had felt. Something in the forest had woken with the arrival of the children.

None of this made sense to the cat. But making sense of things had never been of any particular interest to Corisander.

He felt the flow of an ancient spirit and he didn't sleep that night.

CHAPTER SIX

THE OLD KING

Unseen. Unheard. Nowhere. Everywhere. Without mind, and yet there were memories like distant veils of fog. Without heart, and yet there were moments of agony and joy. He was nothing and he was everything. He was the tree that stood tall and the tree that lay decaying. He was the leaf in all of its colors. He was the bluebell in spring and the mushroom in autumn. He was the branch and the twig and the root and he was the earth in between.

He saw nothing, he heard nothing, understood nothing … and felt everything. Echoes of feverish dreams. What he felt that day was different.

Something had changed.

Something, someone, had come and for the first time in millennia he remembered himself. They had called him the Old King.

And the Old King stirred.

CHAPTER SEVEN

ROBERT THE ARCHER

Roberta was up at sunrise. This had always been her way and it had been the way of her family. It was in that early time that the forest gave its gifts. And it was also the time when the forest was safest. Still, they had never entered the forest unarmed and Roberta wasn't about to change that now. She was determined to stay alive until the lump within her finished her off.

She had pulled aside the fence behind the shed and now steadily, silently, stalked through the forest. She had always loved Wychwood. The dangers, the excitement, the hunts, the fights – but also the calm and beauty of it all. Every bush, every berry, every flower and every bark of every tree. Even in old age she would sometimes sit and look at one single thing for hours on end. With the changing lights of the day, a blackberry could glow with the colors of the world.

Roberta took another step, stopped, listened. The first birds came alive. She couldn't see them, but she heard the first calls of treecreepers and nuthatches. A squirrel up ahead, rushing up a tree. When the birds fell silent, Roberta gripped her fingers tightly around the hatchet in her right hand. She stood, immobile, her eyes closed. Her ears had saved her life more than once. Finally, the first of the birds sang again. Roberta relaxed her hand. It was time to head back. She had a lot to prepare for what she intended to be a very special day for the children. She picked up the basket filled with twigs, flowers, roots and berries and left Wychwood as silently as she had entered it.

When Milo entered the kitchen, Ellie and Nick were seated at the table and Roberta just added another dish containing sausages to the table decorated with leaves and flowers and filled with omelets, porridge, rolls, jams and more. Roberta watched Milo closely as he squinted against the bright sunlight that streaked across the room.

"Grandma's made breakfast for us," Ellie announced with her mouth full.

"Hmn," Milo said, sitting down.

The cat entered the room. Roberta gave Corisander a light nod and the cat seemed to return it, then took up its usual spot on the window sill.

"Good morning, Milo," Roberta said. "Did you sleep all right?"

"Sure," Milo mumbled with a glance at her. He looked at the offerings on the table, then down at his feet. There were no bandages. Roberta had gone to his room early in the morning, had removed them and had seen that the scratches were almost healed. All that was left were faint scars, barely visible to the eye. Roberta Kibble's Famous Healing Balm to the rescue, Roberta thought to herself with a smile. He seemed to have slept all right and last night's sleepwalking obviously didn't concern him.

"That's wonderful," Roberta said, giving him a knowing

wink. "It's the fresh air, you know. Why don't you join your brother and sister and have a bit of breakfast. You must be starving."

"I really am," Milo said as if only just realizing now. He sat down, loaded his plate and soon the three of them were grinning at each other as they raced for every final bit of every plate until not a single thing was left to eat.

"Anything else I can offer you? Roberta asked.

"I would explode," Ellie said happily.

"No thanks," Milo added.

"I'm okay," Nick said. Something was on his mind, Roberta could tell by the way he didn't look at her. "Grandma," he continued. "Why didn't Mom want to come back here?"

"Ah, yes," Roberta said, took her cup of tea and sat down at the table. They looked at her expectantly. Roberta leaned forward. "Wychwood has long been a royal forest and that meant that only the king and those favored by him were allowed to kill deer and cut wood. Men called foresters, woodwards and rangers were put in charge to enforce the king's law and punish those acting against it."

Roberta saw that Nick was getting annoyed, his question unanswered. She lightly smiled and lifted her hands to signal for patience.

"You will understand soon enough, Nick. This is your tale, Children. In the year of sixteen hundred and ninety-nine, during the reign of King William III, a man named Robert came to Wychwood. They say he came from Ireland, a stranger with a bow, a quiver full of arrows and the eyes of an eagle. Robert joined the king's rangers and soon became known, and feared. He was a plain man, honest and hard. Poachers were right to fear him."

"What's a poacher?" Ellie asked.

"Someone who hunts and catches animals where he's not allowed to," Roberta explained, then continued. "One day Robert came across a band of seven poachers. They had already killed and half-skinned a deer when he found them. In the fight that followed, Robert killed four of them, two more he left alive and bound them to a tree. Those two laughed and told Robert that he had lost despite the fight, because the seventh poacher had run off with the deer on his back at the start of the fight. This didn't seem to worry Robert in the least. He calmly took a single arrow from his quiver and shot it, in one swift motion, into the deep of the forest. The arrow disappeared between the trees and the poachers laughed ever louder. But their laughter stopped when they heard a scream. You see, Robert had shot that arrow through the densest of forests and that one arrow killed the seventh poacher."

"Another Wychwood tale," Nick said, trying not to sound impressed.

"Yes, another tale," Roberta said and smiled. "Robert then unbound the two thieves and they walked a good five minutes through thick undergrowth until they found the seventh poacher dead, with the arrow stuck precisely in the center of his neck. From that day forth he was called Robert the Archer."

"Cool story," Milo said.

"Yes, but I don't get what it has to do with Mom," Nick replied.

"I wasn't always a Kibble, Children," Roberta said conspiratorially. Without meaning to, all three children leaned forward. "You see, before I married Henry Kibble and became Roberta Kibble, I was Roberta Archer."

The children looked at her in confusion for a moment, then realization swept across their faces.

"You're related to Robert the Archer?" Ellie asked in wonder.

"We are all related to Robert the Archer, my dear Ellie," Roberta said. "In fact, the three of you are the last of the Archers. And that's why Lily moved away ... because being an Archer is dangerous business."

"What business?" Nick asked intently.

"Kids!" Andrew called from outside.

"I will tell you everything," Roberta said, whispering now. "I will tell you about the world beyond the fence. I will tell you about the life of an Archer. I will tell you about the dangers and the joys, Children," Roberta said as she rose. "But you have to promise to keep it all a secret."

"I can't tell Dad?" Ellie asked.

"Especially not your father," Roberta said grimly. "All of this can end now, before it begins, with a fairytale about a man called Robert the Archer. But if you want to know more, I must have your promise."

"Hey Kids, you have to see this!" Andrew called again.

Roberta stood, waiting, looking at them. She knew she was asking a lot from the children. But she also knew that

Andrew would take them away from here the moment he knew any of what she would reveal to them. She saw an eagerness in Milo's eyes.

"I promise," he said.

Nick frowned at Milo, then shrugged.

"Okay," he said.

"Okay what?" Roberta asked evenly.

"I promise," Nick grumbled.

Ellie looked from Nick to Milo and back to Nick.

"Are you sure?" Ellie asked him.

"No big deal, Ellie," Nick said lightly.

"… I promise, too," Ellie finally said.

"Good. That's settled then," Roberta said with a decisive nod. "We'll begin right after you've gone to see your father."

"What's he doing?" Nick asked.

"Well, go see for yourself," Roberta said, lightly smiling.

CHAPTER EIGHT

THE HAPPY PLACE

Corisander watched the children walk out into the garden behind the house. He remained on the window sill for now as the children looked around, calling for their father.

They couldn't see him and neither could the cat. But Corisander knew all the same.

He sat up and looked across the kitchen to the old woman standing by the sink.

Everything Roberta had been moments earlier, in the company of the children, had disappeared. She had maintained the vigor, the voice and the smile in their presence.

Now it was gone.

Corisander saw that death was approaching her. It wouldn't be long until her final breath and he wondered how she would still find the strength to train them.

Roberta coughed and tried to stifle it. Corisander watched her swallow something from a bottle. Both weak and angry, she defiantly straightened her back, took a twig from an open jar and began chewing on it vigorously.

"I'm not done just yet," Roberta said to the cat. With that she put on a smile. "Let's go see what they're up to out there."

Corisander jumped from the sill and followed Roberta out into the garden, where Nick and Milo stood. Nick was clearly annoyed, arms crossed.

Milo kept turning, looking everywhere. Then Ellie ran from behind the shed, her face flushed.

"I can't find him," she exclaimed.

"I'm too old for hide and seek, Dad," Nick called.

"Me, too," Milo said. "Grandma," he continued with a whisper, "where's he hiding?"

"I haven't the faintest idea," Roberta said as her eyes went up.

Instantly they all looked up and spotted their father sitting high up in the beech tree, grinning down at them. Next to him sat Lily, her face blank as always, her legs dangling.

"Took you long enough," Andrew said.

"How did you get up there?" Milo asked.

"Check out the other side of the tree," Andrew replied.

Corisander sat next to Roberta in the damp grass.

He felt through the earth and the air and the trees beyond.

There was peace.

A badger not far away, a fox and her litter in a hole just beyond the fence, birds, squirrels, mice … nothing else.

Corisander watched the children disappear behind the wide trunk of the beech tree to the left. He heard them discovering the old step ladder, then climbing up one after the other. He felt their excitement as they rose higher with every step.

If things were to go according to their grandmother's plans, the children would soon experience excitement – and dangers – far beyond climbing trees.

Moments later, Nick, then Milo, sat down next to their parents on either side. Ellie joined them last and remained standing, not holding on to anything, looking perfectly at ease. The children discovered countless ribbons, in all sorts of faded colors, wrapped around many of the branches and swaying in the light breeze.

"Sit down, Ellie," Andrew said.

"I love it up here," Ellie replied and remained standing as if she hadn't heard.

"Ellie, it's dangerous, please sit down," Andrew repeated.

"I don't think you'll have to worry, Andrew," Roberta called up. "If Ellie is anything like her mother, she'll be just fine. Lily used to be up there, tree-jumping all the time. She called it the Happy Place."

"Tree-jumping," Ellie said with a beaming smile as she lightly jumped from one branch to another and steadied herself effortlessly.

"Ellie!" Andrew called out in fear.

The girl swung around a vertical branch, then sat down in one gracefully fluid motion. As she did, Corisander wondered once more. The girl's sense of balance was more than unusual.

"Sorry, Dad," Ellie said, trying not to grin too broadly. "It's just so beautiful up here. Grandma, did Mom put the ribbons here?"

"Every single one of them," Grandma called up. "Are you all feeling all right up there? Nobody afraid of heights?"

"Not this bunch," Andrew said with pride in his voice. "They were climbing up everything before they could walk properly."

"Good. Good," Roberta mumbled to herself as she checked her watch. "All right, then, Children. It's time."

"Time for what?" Andrew asked.

"Oh, I've promised to show them around Finstock."

"I can drive you," Andrew said, getting to his feet. "You shouldn't exert yourself."

"Sit down," Roberta said sternly. She took a deep breath, then smiled up into the tree again. "Yes, I will die. Until then I shall go on living. Don't worry, the walk, the fresh air, the company of the children, it'll all do me good. You just keep an eye on Lily. And we, well, we shall go and explore."

CHAPTER NINE

A VISIT TO THE DEAD

Roberta led the way as they walked along Witney Road toward the center of Finstock.

She smiled to herself. Finstock had always been small and anyone passing by along Witney Road could miss it if blinking at the wrong moment. There was a church, a cemetery and a miniscule village shop that served, at the same time, also as the post office. Beyond the road Finstock had a small village hall and, at the bottom of the hill, the village's only pub, The Plough. A village unnoticed by the world.

"We're almost there," Roberta said over her shoulder. They were walking single file along the narrow road that was flanked by tall hedges. Nick walked behind her, then came Ellie and Milo … and finally there was Corisander.

"Where is there?" Nick asked.

"Cemetery," Roberta replied. She glanced back when another car rushed past them and saw Ellie giving the cat a worried glance. "Don't worry about Corisander, Ellie. He comes with me all the time."

"Why are we going to the cemetery?" Milo asked.

"You'll see soon enough," Roberta replied.

They passed the Cowley farm on the right, a house in bad repair. Two dogs in a kennel, barking. A rusty tractor stood in the yard, its hood open and a man peering inside and cursing.

"Morning, Gordon!" Roberta called across the street.

Gordon Cowley looked up from his work. He was a thin man, sinewy and unshaven. When he saw Roberta and the kids he grunted a hello, then bent over the engine again.

"That was Gordon Cowley," Roberta said as they walked on. "Always a rough sort but in his heart he used to be quite a nice man. Gordon lost his wife a long time ago and his children have moved away ... so it goes."

On the left of the street, behind the fence, Wychwood followed them for a while. Roberta had walked this way a thousand times. She knew every bush, every rock, every sign and every crack in the road. She knew the trees beyond the hedges and the changing smells of the elder and the hawthorn. A ten-minute walk from the house to the village center and it felt like ten hours to Roberta. Where Wychwood ended, the fields began and the skies became wide. Roberta stopped and grabbed hold of a wooden fence that surrounded the field.

"Are you okay, Grandma?" Nick asked.

"Sure, just give me a moment." Roberta caught her breath, then pointed at a church steeple up ahead. "See? Like I said, almost there."

On the right side of the street was a small property, a house in decent enough condition, but the yard was filled with piles of wood and metal. Several monstrous sculptures made from scrap metal surrounded the house.

"Who lives there?" Ellie asked.

"Christopher Smith," Roberta said. "He's a retired policeman. They call him Nutter Smith around here because, well, he's quite eccentric."

Roberta smiled at the children, then took another deep breath before she let go of the fence and continued on.

A few minutes later Roberta entered through the gate and led the children past the church to the cemetery beyond. The small graveyard was, in part, shaded by immense walnut trees. Gravestones old and new, straight and crooked, small and massive, rose from the ground in uneven lanes.

"Let's see then," Roberta said. "Can any of you tell me where the Archers lie?"

Ellie instantly took off, looking at one gravestone after another, silently reading name after name on large stones with crosses and angel statues, square blocks with nothing but simple carvings and rough rocks with metal plaques. Nick remained next to Roberta, scanning the surroundings while Milo walked straight toward the back of the cemetery.

"What do you think?" Roberta asked Nick.

"I think Milo's got it," Nick said, pointing to where Milo was heading.

"Here!" Milo called.

Ellie ran to Milo and Nick followed with Roberta. Roberta didn't need to look for the cat.

Corisander never entered the cemetery. The cat usually slept on one of the sun-warmed stone walls outside the church ground. The graves of the Archers, two long rows, were separate from the rest of the villagers by an empty lane of grass. Roberta walked them to the first stone on the far left.

"Why are the Archers buried apart from the other villagers?" Ellie asked quietly.

"No need to whisper, Ellie. They're all dead, you know," Roberta said with a smile. The smile disappeared when she continued. "Your ancestors were buried here because they were both feared and respected, always. You see, they were protecting the forest but there was something more to them and it all began with Robert the Archer."

They stood in front of a withered stone that was partially covered by a thick layer of ivy.

The name "Robert the Archer" was chiseled in simple letters and, beneath it, the information that he had been born in 1673 and had died in 1758.

"Robert protected the king's forest. But sometimes he would disappear in the forest and not return for weeks. What began with Robert, continued through the generations. The Archers spent more time in the forest than they spent with people and so the villagers began to talk about them. Stories sprang up about the strange clan of the Archers and in some of them the Archers even became witches and conjurors of dark spirits. None of this is true, of course," Roberta added quickly, when she saw the worried look on Ellie's face. "The Archers were always true to their word and upheld the law. And so, despite the stories of the feared and dangerous Archers, they were respected for keeping the peace in the forest."

"Why did he disappear in the forest?" Milo asked.

"What did he do in there for weeks?" Nick added.

"He found friends … and he found enemies," Roberta said.

At that moment the church bell rang out with what always sounded to Roberta like the complaint of a whiny old tin man. Good timing, Roberta thought.

"Children, I have choir practice," she said to their surprise. Roberta had planned it this way. She wanted them to get used to the idea of the Archers. She wanted them to think about it, to be with their ancestors. Training would begin soon enough. As she walked away from them toward the church, she called back. "I'll see you at the house in an hour."

CHAPTER TEN

FOUR HUNDRED
AND SEVENTY-ONE

Corisander saw Roberta wave once more before entering the church. Churches. Nothing wrong with them. Nothing wrong with anything unless people squared the rounds and they had, over the past three thousand years, shown an increasing aptitude to do just that.

He lay on the wall and watched a butterfly land a few feet away in a spot warmed by the rays of the sun. Corisander felt the change in the air as the wings of the butterfly came to a rest. What beautiful creatures. Humans called that one a Red Admiral. Wings flat against the stone, the butterfly seemed asleep. Maybe it was, maybe it wasn't. Maybe that butterfly was like Corisander. While Corisander sensed a lot, he didn't, couldn't, sense everything. There was mystery left even for him.

He watched the children and heard them quite clearly as they walked from one grave to the next, wondering about their ancestors.

"So they were all protecting the forest?" Ellie asked.

"According to Grandma, yes," Nick said.

"I want to know what's in the forest," Milo said.

"Animals and trees. And that's that," Nick said.

"But Grandma says Robert the Archer found friends in the forest, and enemies," Ellie replied.

"Grandma says a lot of things and nothing much," Nick said, irritated. "Look Ellie, she's an old woman and she's – ... Let's just ... humor her."

"You saw the pictures in my room," Ellie said.

"What pictures?" Milo asked.

"Pictures of our family, old, young, men, women – and they all carry bows and arrows and axes and knives," Ellie said.

"Protectors of the forest," Milo said, more to himself.

"Oh, please," Nick said.

"Watch it," Milo said, mock-serious, staring up at Nick. "Don't mess with an Archer."

"You're an idiot," Nick said and couldn't help smiling.

"Yes, but I'm an Archer idiot. I'm a strange Archer, a dangerous Archer and a feared Archer so you better watch it."

Ellie laughed out loud and the others joined in, too. When they left the cemetery moments later, Corisander jumped off the wall. He listened to the choir struggling through some ominous sounding piece of music, then followed the children. Roberta Kibble could take care of herself. As for the children, Corisander wasn't quite that certain and so decided to accompany them on their way back home.

For a while the children walked in silence. On their way to the cemetery they had not seen a single villager. Now on their return that found themselves the center of attention.

Corisander knew them all, of course. Harriet Thorne greeted them, as she passed on the other side of the road, with a curt smile and suspicion in her eyes. The thin woman with a nose like a hawk's beak was manager of the village shop and felt herself the village guardian, keeping an eye on everything and everyone. She didn't recognize the children and yet, they did look oddly familiar. Thomas Crawford looked up from his rose bushes as they passed and he kept his eyes on them until they were gone from sight. The old man remembered the Archers and those kids were Archers without a doubt. Corisander felt the old man's pulse quicken.

"Everybody's watching us," Ellie said under her breath.

"Well, we're strangers," Nick said with a shrug.

"Archer strangers," Milo said evenly, making them all smile again.

Occasionally Corisander wished he could talk. Right at that moment he would have told the children to step behind the hedge because trouble was coming. Trouble in the form of former police constable Christopher Smith. The tall man was Roberta's age and was as wiry as the bicycle he rode on. He rode past them and then they heard the bicycle brakes screech.

"Wait!" Smith shouted.

The children looked at each other and turned around. They stood side by side as the old man turned and stopped inches from them. Corisander sat down to the side, watching closely. He could feel the excitement and fear and genuine concern whirling within the old man. Smith showed none of it.

"Who are you?" Smith said gruffly.

"Who are you?" Milo replied like a shot. Smith glared at him, then nodded.

"Rude of me, you're right, young man, you're quite right. I'm Police Constable Christopher Smith and you are?"

"Aren't you a bit old to be a policeman?" Nick asked.

"I'm retired, of course," Smith said begrudgingly.

"So, you're not a policeman anymore," Milo said.

Ellie rolled her eyes and stepped in.

"We're the Murphys, Mr. Smith and we're here visiting our grandmother Roberta Kibble."

"My God," Smith said, staring at them. "Just as I thought, you're Archers."

"Yes, we are," Milo said proudly.

Smith looked at them in silence for a moment. Then he got off his bicycle, put it on its stand and addressed the children once more, every bit of gruffness gone from his face.

"How long will you be there?"

"Why?" Nick asked.

"You're right. You're right, of course, none of my business. It's just that – I'm afraid for your lives, children. Whatever you do, do not go into the forest."

Corisander sat and watched, nothing to be done.

He was quite aware of what Christopher Smith was about to import. What he knew and what he thought he knew.

It wasn't going to make Roberta's plan any easier.

Corisander saw the children glance at each other, then at the old man again.

"The forest's private anyway," Nick said.

"That doesn't stop everybody," Smith replied gravely. "Do not enter the forest."

"Why not?" Milo asked, his question a challenge.

"Wychwood is full of evil," Smith began, a fire burning in his eyes. "Bad things happen because of this forest, as they have happened to your ancestors. I have put together a list of four hundred and seventy-one people who have disappeared in Wychwood forest."

Corisander wasn't surprised that the children didn't leave. Smith delivered his words with intensity, something he had acquired since his retirement, something that had left him alone in old age. Corisander knew the story of Police Constable Christopher Smith who had lost his son to the forest. Smith had lived, together with his wife and only child, his son Matthew, in Finstock. They had known the stories and they had stayed away from the forest. Until one day Matthew was gone. They found one of his sneakers by the edge of the forest and that was all they ever found. Smith organized search parties with reluctant villagers, who agreed to search only outside of the forest, and police assistance from Witney and Oxford who entered Wychwood. A dozen constables joined three Oakham Park Estate rangers, combed the forest in every possible way and found nothing but treacherous roots, thick undergrowth, thorny bushes and startled deer. They left Wychwood bruised, scraped and torn.

For the following weeks and months Smith had organized further searches, had involved radio and television and saw how the villagers nodded. They understood. They had all lost someone to the forest – or at least knew someone who had. They knew that little Matthew would never be found. They knew that eventually Police Constable Christopher Smith would have to give up the search and move on with his life. Smith's way of dealing with the loss was unusual. He quit his job and continued to search in every way he could think of and when there was no hope of finding his son he focused on the forest. He began to research and compile – old stories, personal accounts, distant memories. As the years went on he became known in the villages surrounding Wychwood as "Nutter Smith", a loony old man, driven to believe even the most ridiculous of tales.

"At first I thought that it had something to do with the owners of Wychwood forest, the Thorntons, or their rangers. But this is far more frightening. Do you understand what I'm saying?" Smith said, taking another step toward the children.

"I think we should go," Nick said.

"Four hundred and seventy-one," Smith repeated. "And those are just the ones I managed, through years of intensive research, to uncover. There are bound to be more, many more, who have disappeared in the years before there were records."

Nick turned to leave and Ellie was eager to follow, but Milo didn't move.

"What do you think has happened to all those people?" Milo asked.

"I don't know," Smith said. "There's no proof, just stories and fairytales and hundreds if not thousands of people vanished forever. I think … I believe … that there are some kind of monsters in Wychwood."

"Let's go, Milo, please," Ellie said.

"What kind of monsters?" Nick asked, curious now.

"I don't know … but it's the only explanation." The old man saw that he had sufficiently worried the children. He turned the bicycle and mounted it. "Do not enter the forest, Children," he said once more and rode off toward the village shop.

"Meow," Corisander said when they kept staring after the old man. Ellie bent down and stroked his back and Corisander showed his appreciation with a profound purr.

"What a weirdo," Nick said as they continued their walk back.

"What if he's right?" Milo asked.

"The Archers made friends and enemies in the forest," Ellie added.

"I have no intention of going in there anyway," Nick said, trying to sound casual.

"I have," Milo said. "I have even dreamed about it."

Milo recounted the dream, the jumping and flying, the squirrels, the boar – and the moving forest. Suddenly the boys noticed that Ellie had stopped walking.

"What?" Nick asked.

"I've been dreaming, too," Ellie said uncomfortably. "I

was in the forest, just like Milo."

"Damn ..." Nick said, his brow furrowed. "I never remember my dreams but now that you two mention it – I think I've been in the forest, too."

As they walked they wondered about the strange dreams but also how much they had loved being in the forest. They soon saw Wychwood rise to the right, appearing and disappearing behind the road's tall hedges. Corisander felt the pull just as he knew the children felt it.

"Do you feel it?" Milo asked.

"It feels like something's telling me to go in there," Ellie replied.

"Let's shut up about it. It's a bunch of trees and that's that. We'll talk to Grandma when she's back," Nick said. He had felt it, too, and he felt it right at that moment. He gave Ellie a carefree smile that vanished the moment he faced front again.

CHAPTER ELEVEN

A BASKET OF KNIVES

Roberta had always been fond of the people of Finstock. She greatly appreciated how very different they were from herself – they were, for the most part, entirely ordinary. When one lived the life of an Archer, the ordinary occasionally was welcome relief. Choir practice had been as horrid as it had always been. Roberta could never understand why people enjoyed standing inside dark and damp buildings while attempting to wring a drop of beauty from dreadful songs and melodies. But whenever she had been there, front row far left, she had contentedly smiled. The company of the ordinary.

She hadn't told anyone in Finstock about her impending death. Dealing with the cancer was bad enough. Dealing with the villagers' whispers and glances and offers of care and help would be entirely intolerable. George Payne, a retired carpenter, dropped her off at the house and, as always, tried his best to charm her into a date.

"There's a dance over in Witney on Saturday," he said casually as he pulled into the yard in front of her house.

"I'm sure you'll have a wonderful time, George," Roberta said and stepped out.

"I'm a good dancer, Roberta," George Payne added, smiling up at her.

"I'm sure you are," she replied, ending the conversation by closing the door. She waved and smiled as he drove off. When she turned, the children were standing there. It was obvious that they had been waiting for her. Roberta took a deep breath.

"Where are your parents?"

"Dad left a note saying they went for a walk," Nick replied.

"We're on our own then. Good," Roberta said evenly. "Come with me."

Roberta walked around the house, walked past the back door and continued straight to the shed. Halfway to the shed, she stopped and the children stopped next to her.

"That's a good distance," Roberta muttered.

"We met Nutter Smith," Nick said.

"Oh, did you?" Roberta said. "Did he tell you not to enter the forest?"

"Yes," Milo said.

"Did he talk about hundreds of missing people?

"Yes," Ellie said quietly.

"Did he tell you about monsters in the forest?"

"Yes," Nick said. "He's definitely crazy," he added half-heartedly.

"Oh, no, my dear Nick," Roberta said. "He's far from crazy. He's right."

"About what?" Nick asked.

"He's right about everything," Roberta said. "Wait here."

Without another word, she walked away from them. Explanations would follow if they proved their worth. She took another look back to where the children were standing, looking at each other, looking at the forest just beyond the shed. Roberta found herself hesitating. Right now, they were innocent. Right now, they were as ordinary as the people of Finstock. But they are also Archers, she said to herself and with that, stepped around the corner and entered the shed.

When she returned, she saw the cat sitting next to the children. Roberta smiled, then focused on the task at hand.

Taking a bit of chalk from her pocket, she drew a circle the size of a head on the weathered wooden wall of the shed. Then she walked back to the children, carrying a heavy basket full of knives and setting it down before them.

"What's with the knives?" Nick asked suspiciously. He frowned at the variety of some thirty knives of different weights and sizes, some with rugged wooden grips, some elegantly bound in leather. Milo and Ellie were already on their knees, examining them.

"Careful, Children – they're razor sharp," Roberta said before turning to Nick. "Nick, the answers to your questions lie beyond those knives. Throw them." With that she pointed at the chalk circle on the wall of the shed some thirty feet from them.

"Not my thing," Nick said.

"How does it work?" Milo asked, balancing a glimmering blade in his hand.

Roberta said nothing. She looked at Milo, then at Ellie. There was something, Roberta could see it in their eyes.

Show me what you can do, Roberta said silently, hoping fervently. She gave Milo a nod to just give it a try. Milo took a deep breath, took the knife by its tip and hurled it at the shed. The knife buried itself into the wood just a foot below the circle with a loud and hollow thud.

"Good," Roberta acknowledged. "Now you, Ellie."

"I've never thrown a knife," Ellie said.

"Don't think about it," Roberta replied.

"You can do it," Milo added, his face glowing with excitement.

Ellie selected a slim knife with a leather handle. Milo nodded encouragingly while Nick gave her nothing but a shrug. She hurled the knife and buried it two feet from the circle.

"Excellent," Roberta said. "Nick?"

"I'm not throwing knives. This is stupid. Whatever you're saying, I'm definitely not going into that forest. I'm not crazy."

He walked away to the patio and sat down, his arms crossed. Roberta gave the others a nod and slowly walked back to Nick. Behind her, she heard knife after knife hitting the shed. Not a single one of them failed to stick. Archers, Roberta thought proudly as she sat down next to Nick. In silence, they watched Milo and Ellie throw knife after knife, laughing, exhilarated.

"Did you know that I had a brother?" Roberta asked Nick.

When Nick looked at her, frowning, he saw that she had two knives in her hands. She threw one of them straight up in the air where it twirled several times, then caught it effortlessly with the same hand.

"I … I think so. Chester?"

"Yes, Chester. Chester Archer. Did you see my brother's grave?"

Nick frowned and Roberta knew that, in his mind, he walked from grave to grave once more, trying to find the name.

"He wasn't there," Nick said. "He's still alive?"

"Oh, he's dead all right. Chester's been dead for a long time … but I can't bury him."

"I don't understand," Nick said in confusion.

"And you won't ever understand until you show me what you can do," Roberta said grimly. She threw her knife straight up once more and again caught it with ease. Roberta held out the other knife for Nick to take.

"I'm not going to throw knives," Nick said again.

"I can't bury my brother because his head is still in the forest," Roberta said.

"What? What are you –?"

"They cut off Chester's head, Nick. Throw it," Roberta said. She rose, her voice deep and forceful as she looked down at Nick. "Throw the knife, Nick."

"Who? What are you talking about?" Nick asked, more and more flustered.

"I'm talking about headhunters," Roberta said severely. "You're a warrior, a protector of Wychwood. Now throw the knife!"

Nick suddenly rose and took the knife, his face flushed,

his body shaking. He was about to walk to the others, when Roberta took his arm.

"From here," she said. Nick stared at her in disbelief, the distance more than twice that of the others. "Trust your senses, Nick. You're an Archer."

Nick shook his head. He was acutely aware of Milo and Ellie watching them, standing aside, waiting. Roberta watched him feel the weight of the knife in his hand and then she watched him change. His body stopped shaking as complete calm washed over him. He lifted his arm and flung the knife. It flew fast and straight and buried itself in the center of the circle with a loud boom.

"Holy crap, Nick, bulls-eye!" Milo shouted.

Roberta had seen enough, more than she had hoped to see, in fact. In anticipation of the return of Andrew and Lily, they hid the knives back in the shed and then settled onto the patio with Roberta Kibble's Famous Afternoon Tea. Roberta watched Milo and Ellie, their conversation animated, the excitement of throwing knives still fresh in their blood. And Roberta watched Nick, sitting there in utter calm, as if meditating. They all had what it took and Nick, Nick had something more.

"Training will begin tomorrow," Roberta said. She felt tired, worn but content. She remembered her first trainings in the forest and she had been younger than Ellie. They would be fine. Surely they would be fine as long as they did as they were told.

"We all dreamed about being in the forest last night," Ellie said.

Roberta felt herself frown and quickly made sure none of her concern showed. How could they have all dreamed the same dream?

"You need not worry about it, dear ones," Roberta said as earnestly and casually as she could. "Such Wychwood dreams are not uncommon."

"All at the same time?" Nick asked.

"I told you, Wychwood is a wondrous place."

"Tell us about the headhunters," Nick said and Roberta heard him as if from far away.

"Headhunters?" Milo asked through thick, white fog.

"Meow," the cat said and jumped into Roberta's lap. "Meow."

Roberta tried to speak but the words wouldn't come. She reached for her cup of tea and sent it crashing to the ground. She looked for the children and saw them disappearing in a whirling fog. No, not now. I can't die yet. I won't die yet.

Willing control to her fingers, she took an ornamented key from her pocket and pushed it into Nick's hand. She heard the children's voices, vibrating with fear, from far away.

Help, Roberta screamed inside her head.

The last thing she saw were the cat's eyes.

CHAPTER TWELVE

THE ARMORY
AND THE SKELETON

Corisander had done his best to steady the racing minds of the children. To his surprise they had reacted admirably, with Ellie and Milo taking care of their unconscious grandmother and Nick managing to alert emergency services. Their parents returned from the walk just in time to see the yellow ambulance arrive with lights flashing and sirens wailing.

Andrew had handed over responsibility for Lily to the children, then watched the emergency nurse assess the situation. He explained the cancer and the doctor's diagnosis and the nurse gravely nodded as they lifted Roberta onto a stretcher. Within less than two minutes, Roberta was pushed into the back of the ambulance.

"Are you coming along?" the nurse asked Andrew, holding the door open.

"Kids?" Andrew said, turning to look at them.

"We're okay," Nick said.

Andrew fixed his eyes on one after the other and, one by one, they all nodded.

"Keep an eye on your mother," Andrew said. He gave them a brave smile, hugged Ellie quickly, then jumped into the back of the ambulance. The nurse closed the door, then paused and stepped to the children.

"Your grandmother just fainted," she said. "From what I've seen, I believe she will be home again tomorrow, so don't you worry too much." With a nod and a smile she hurried away. The ambulance, lights still flashing, kicked up gravel and dust as it drove out of sight.

Half an hour later, the children still hadn't spoken.

Corisander saw Nick sitting in one of the garden chairs, blankly staring at the target circle on the wall of the shed. Milo was up in Lily's Happy Place, his legs dangling, his eyes on the forest. Ellie held her mother's hand and walked in slow circles around the boulders in the garden.

The carvings on those boulders, placed there by Roberta's late husband … they were swirls of the flow, obvious to Corisander's eyes and remarkable that the stone mason had apparently seen them for himself. Maybe in his dreams, maybe floating in the air? Corisander would likely never now but he was certain that the life of Henry Kibble was another tale worthy of Wychwood Forest. Roberta's husband had died thirty years ago, killed by a falling gargoyle while he was working at Oakham Park House. Corisander had never met Henry Kibble, but he was certain that he would have very much liked the man.

When he jumped onto the chair next to Nick, Corisander saw that the boy was holding the key his grandmother had pushed into his hands. Absent-mindedly, he turned it around and around.

For a while the words and stories Roberta had told them

had been pushed aside. Now they flooded back. Nick got to his feet and when he did, the others looked his way.

"What?" Milo called down from the tree.

"I have to tell you something," Nick said. Milo swiftly climbed off the tree and Ellie circled the last boulder with her mother, then placed her in a chair.

Corisander saw Nick struggle as he recalled the heated moments with his grandmother. Then he told Milo and Ellie everything she had told him. That the Archers were warriors, that there were some sort of headhunters in the forest, that they had cut off the head of Grandma's brother. Nick told them how upset she was when telling him that she couldn't bury her brother because his head was still in the forest.

Corisander looked at them and looked at Lily, too. They had not noticed it, but Lily's lip had twitched at the mention of the headhunters. Corisander had never seen as dense a fog as the one that clouded Lily's mind. But something was happening in there. Somewhere, somewhere deep within Lily, something was stirring. Maybe it was memories. Maybe it was a mother's love … maybe it was a mother's fear.

"This is all nuts," Milo said.

"There are headhunters in the forest? Headhunters?" Ellie asked fearfully.

"I don't know," Nick said. "None of this makes sense, true. But remember the cop telling us about all the missing people?"

Milo and Ellie nodded.

"And we're throwing knives like pros," Milo added.

Ellie looked at the forest beyond the fence. It seemed as if Wychwood was doing its best to appear cheerful and bright. The light of the sun streaked deep into the forest, turning the usual dark green into a sparkling gleam.

"There is no way I'll ever go in there," Ellie said.

"Of course we're not going in there," Nick exclaimed and, when Milo said nothing, turned to him. "Right?"

"I don't know," Milo replied, surprising the others. "We're Archers. We're protectors of the forest, whatever that means. We throw knives. We're supposed to be warriors."

"We're not going in there," Nick said again.

"What makes you think you're safe out here?" Milo asked. "If there are headhunters in the forest, do you really think that fence stops them?"

"Grandma wouldn't live here if it wasn't safe," Nick said, trying to sound certain. When Milo was about to go on, Nick held up the key. "She gave it to me just before she fell unconscious. I think she gave it to me because she thought she was going to die."

Ellie took it from Nick, turned it around, her fingers tracing the ornaments.

"What do you think it's for?"

"Let's find out," Milo said eagerly.

Corisander could see their spirits lifted by Milo's excitement at the thought of uncovering the mysteries behind the door that key would unlock. Corisander jumped into Lily's lap and closed his eyes as the children searched the house from the cellar to the attic.

In the house, there was nothing that would require that particular key, they would discover that soon enough. Corisander felt Lily's hand softly stroking his fur. Through the thick gray mist of her mind, Corisander tried to send her swirls of colors. In the scheme of things, it didn't matter. Lily would live and then she would die. The children would talk and dance and laugh with her … or they would not. Within moments of Corisander's life, they would be gone and his life would continue.

And yet, he wanted Lily to return … and he wanted the children to live.

When they exited the house and walked toward the shed, Corisander opened his eyes. The chances of the children living long lives decreased with every step they took towards that shed.

Corisander jumped to the ground and meowed. Ellie turned and waved for the others to wait. She quickly came to take Lily's hand and took her along.

The inside of the shed contained rusty metal shelves and worn wooden ones. Used clay pots in all shapes and sizes were stacked in the corner and to the side a pile of broken ones lay. Garden tools hung on hooks and stood against the walls and several old wardrobes lined the back of the wall.

It was just a matter of time, Corisander thought.

"Let's try the closets," Milo said and already ran to open them. He was disappointed to find that all of them opened without a key and contained nothing but garden utensils of every variety and dozens of bags of seeds. "Oh, come on," Milo said, clearly frustrated.

"We've looked everywhere," Ellie said. "Maybe the key means something else."

"Maybe," Nick said, his eyes slowly scanning the shed.

"No, there has to be a door," Milo said. "We'll just have to start again. Same thing, every room, tap every wall. Let's go." He was halfway out the shed when Nick stopped him.

"Just wait a second."

"There's nothing here, Nick," Milo said, annoyed. His brother's eyes were fixed on the side wall where rusty rakes and shovels hung on hooks. Milo walked from left to right along the wall and checked and rapped against it. "See? Nothing."

"There's no light," Nick said.

Smart young man, Corisander thought.

Indeed, there were glimmers of sunlight shining through the cracks in three of the four walls of the shed. The fourth wall seemed more solid – no light seemed to manage to penetrate it.

Nick walked along the wall Milo had just inspected and came to the far corner where a wardrobe stood. He opened it and found nothing that would have suggested a hidden door.

"I think Mom doesn't like it in here," Ellie worried. The expression in Lily's face was as blank as it ever was, but she was now lightly swaying.

"Meow," Corisander replied.

"Maybe we shouldn't be here," Ellie suggested. "Maybe

Mom remembers something about this place. Let's just leave it."

"I think there's an inner and an outer wall," Nick announced, ignoring Ellie.

"Let me check," Milo said, picking up an old pickaxe.

"Are you nuts? Just, hold on," Nick demanded, annoyed. He tried to move the wardrobe but it didn't budge. It was Ellie who discovered that one of the hooks on the wall seemed almost polished in one spot, as if it had been more used than the others. When she pulled it, the wardrobe swung back and revealed a heavy wooden door.

"Awesome," Milo exclaimed in a hush.

As if in slow-motion, Lily turned and began walking out of the shed. Ellie took her by the hand and brought her back as Nick stepped forward and inserted the key. The lock clicked open and, with a glance at his brother and sister, Nick opened the door.

"What do you see?" Milo whispered.

"Nothing much," Nick replied. He very slowly took a step forward to see around the corner and discovered a switch. Electric light flickered on. "There are stairs."

"Let's go," Milo said.

"We don't know what's down there," Nick said cautiously.

"Let's wait for Grandma to come back," Ellie added.

"No way," Milo said and took a step past Nick. Holding on to the pickaxe, he walked down to the bottom of the stairs and disappeared from sight.

"Milo?" Nick called. When no reply came, he turned to

Ellie. "Wait here, don't come down. Stay with Mom, okay? I'll be right back."

As he stepped through the door, Milo's voice, filled with excitement, rang out.

"Holy crap you guys have to see this!"

Corisander knew what was down there. He had been in the armory many times. Down there was a large underground room five times the size of the shed. When the boys came up again, moments later, both of them looking unnaturally pale, Corisander knew that they had discovered more than just weapons down there.

"What? What is it?" Ellie asked. "What's down there?"

"An armory," Nick said, staring at his shoes.

"A what?"

"A weapons room," Nick mumbled.

"Axes, knives, hatchets, lances, crossbows, bows and arrows," Milo said monotonously. "Strange suits, too. There's benches and tools to make weapons and to fix them, I guess. There's also maps of the forest on the wall."

Nick turned off the light, closed the door and locked it. He put the key in his pocket, then pulled the hook. The wardrobe slid back into place.

"What's wrong?" Ellie asked, worried.

Nick and Milo looked at each other.

"I think we also found Grandma's brother down there," Nick finally said.

"There's a skeleton on a table, all there, except for the head," Milo added.

Ellie just stared at them in disbelief.

"Where's Mom?" Nick said suddenly.

"She was right next to me!" Ellie exclaimed and Corisander felt her heart beating at a furious pace.

Nick and Milo raced past her out of the shed.

Corisander cursed himself. Why hadn't he paid attention? Why hadn't he felt her leave?

Lily had to have walked out of the shed with the stealth of a ghost.

"Mom!" Nick shouted.

"Mom!" Milo and Ellie echoed.

Milo charged around the shed while Nick and Ellie ran up and down the fence.

"Check the house!" Nick shouted at Milo. Milo was already halfway there, while Ellie ran around it. Nick took a look up and down Witney Road, then joined Milo in searching the house.

Lily was nowhere in sight.

Corisander meowed as loudly as he could. He ran with them, trying to get them back to the fence, trying to show them the place where Roberta usually lifted it to enter Wychwood.

He watched the children yell at each other, more distressed with every passing second. Milo charged up the tree to Lily's Happy Place but she was nowhere to be found. Of course not, Corisander thought and meowed again.

He charged through Nick's running legs, making him stumble and fall.

"Stupid cat!" Nick yelled at Corisander.

He didn't mind. For just an instant he had the boy's attention. He meowed again and ran to the fence where he sat down, still as a statue, staring at Nick and the others.

Milo frowned, then ran to the spot where Corisander sat. He reached up and down the fence, pulled at it and discovered the opening. He gasped when he realized that his mother might have disappeared into the forest.

"Nick, Ellie!" he yelled and they stood next to him instants later, staring at the opening, frightened by the possibility it presented.

"We have to go in," Milo said and put one leg across to the other side. Nick held him back.

"We don't know that she's in there," Nick said.

"She could be!" Milo yelled at him.

"We have to go in," Ellie said, nodding at Milo.

Corisander looked at their faces. He could see the fear in their eyes.

He could feel their hearts hammering at the thought of their mother being in danger. Corisander knew that they were all thinking of the headhunters.

They were right to be afraid.

CHAPTER THIRTEEN

THE SCENT OF BLOOD

There was nothing to be done and so Corisander sat by the fence and waited. He knew that the children's mother had walked into the forest and he knew the direction she had walked in. There was no way for Corisander to tell them. Untrained and ignorant of the ways of Wychwood, they were still Archers and, Corisander felt, there was even more to them than that. As they crawled through the hole in the fence, they looked at each other.

They felt it, a pulse, a shiver, a ripple that ran through them as they crossed the threshold. To Corisander it was as if the whole of the forest, with every leaf of every tree, had just shuddered and sighed.

Milo was terrified and showed none of it. Neither did Nick and Ellie. Ellie impulsively gave her brothers a fierce embrace, then turned and walked off to the right. The boys nodded at each other, then Nick walked left along the fence and Milo walked straight into the forest.

Within seconds, he couldn't see Nick and Ellie anymore. He was acutely aware of everything around him. He didn't understand it but felt that there were squirrels nearby, and a fox at a distance. At first, the forest seemed silent. No wind in the trees, no birds singing. His every step sounded thunderous to him.

Milo stopped and concentrated. If he had a sense of animals around him, maybe he could sense his mother, too. He heard nothing, sensed nothing. Frustrated, Milo continued. Thorny bushes scratched his arms and legs, he didn't care. Every step took him further away from the fence and deeper into Wychwood. The forest seemed to be darker here, the trees taller, the canopy above blocking out the sunlight. Milo remembered his dream of a forest that had seemed alive.

Without realizing it, Milo made less noise with every step. He instinctively evaded rotting twigs, ducked under clawing branches, stepped across hidden roots. Soon he followed an animal trail in complete silence. When he heard rustling to his left, he froze. His senses tingling, he jumped aside just in time to evade three deer. They crashed into view, seemingly chasing each other. Milo had barely time to notice the spots on their backs and see their white rear ends disappear again. Trying to control his breathing again, Milo realized that his knee was bleeding. Jumping aside he had landed on a root and scraped it badly. He wiped aside the leaves and dirt and got to his feet, ignoring the stinging pain.

The scraped knee brushed against a twig and a single drop of blood remained. The drop hung there for a moment. Below it on the forest floor, unseen by Milo, leaves and twigs, moss and fern moved in silent flow. When the drop of blood fell onto the ground, a shiver rippled through the earth.

Milo frowned, feeling as if he had just been watched. He

was about to go on when he heard the crashing sounds grow louder again. The deer were coming back. Milo hurried to a large oak tree that had a big split in its trunk, an opening big enough to stand in. He stepped into the hollow and waited for the three deer to rush past again.

But the deer didn't come.

Twigs snapped, branches broke and then a creature, unlike any Milo had ever seen, crashed through a bush and stood there, panting. Milo pressed himself further into the hollow of the tree, sinking into its shadow and trying not to breathe. The creature, no taller than Milo, was broad as a bull. He looked filthy, wearing patched clothes that seemed like the forest itself, stained in shades of browns and greens and thickly caked with layers of earth. His short hair seemed to have been cut by the same axe that had hacked the beard, it was ragged and wild as if no brush had ever come close to it. A broad belt held several jagged knives but the creature's huge, claw-like hands carried a pike, a lance with a sharp point and a metal hook at its tip.

Headhunter, was all that Milo could think.

The monstrous little man sniffed the air as he looked around, slowly. Milo's lungs began to seer with pain as he didn't dare to breathe. The headhunter ran one hand through the shaggy reddish-brown beard.

"What are you? You're a strange smell," he said in perfect English and sniffed again. "A boy, but also more than a boy." The creature grinned, exposing foul-looking, pointed teeth. "Well, I thank you for coming to Wychwood."

The headhunter sniffed the air once more, as if savoring the scent, then turned and stepped away from Milo's hiding place. Milo emptied his lungs as quietly as he could, then took another breath. Instantly, the creature turned again.

"You're thinking of running, aren't you, boy?" The headhunter grinned again and took off the dark red cap to wipe his forehead. "But you can't outrun me. I outrun the boar. I am faster than the deer. I can skin a rabbit as it changes direction in mid-air. I am Caark and you, my young friend, you are Caark's prey. Ah, there you are."

Milo couldn't help gasping when the creature stared right at him. Caark stepped closer and stopped right in front of Milo, close enough for him to jerk back from the creature's stench, a mixture of rotting meat and a foul mud hole. As Caark leaned in closer, Milo spotted insects crawling through the creature's beard.

"I'm ... please, I –"

"Please what?" Caark asked. "Please not kill you? Please not taste your blood? Please not eat you?" The creature leered at Milo. "I'm terribly sorry, my boy, but that is exactly what I will be doing."

At that moment, standing rigidly on the outside of the fence, Corisander felt Milo. There was no reason that he should feel the boy, far in the forest, but something extraordinary was happening. Something was waking within the boy.

Milo felt himself shaking and perspiring as the creature stepped ever closer.

"It's been a long while," Caark said. He rammed the pike into the ground, reached for one of the knives in his belt and then added, "Time to die."

The creature wasn't ready for what happened next. How could he be? He had no way of knowing that a boy could do what the boy did. Milo's fist flew out from within the tree and rammed itself into Caark's face. He grabbed his nose, howled, staggered back, then stumbled and fell to the ground.

"What the …," Caark muttered, shaking his head from the blow. As he scrambled back to his feet, Milo was already running. Hoping for his senses to guide him in the right direction, Milo wasted no time in orienting himself. Branches of trees and bushes whipped at him as he flew past. Without realizing it, his eyes picked up everything. He jumped every root, spotted every opening, picked the best route at all times and never lost a moment's worth of speed … and yet the creature was gaining on him.

"I told you, boy. You can't outrun me!"

Milo glanced back. Caark rammed through branches and bushes like a bull, forcing nature to bend and break as he charged forward. When the massive trunk of a fallen tree seemed certain to slow him down, he used the hook of his pike to grab hold of a branch above. Not only did it not slow the headhunter down, the swinging seemed to propel him forward even faster. Milo could almost feel the creature's hand on his neck when he ran out into a clearing.

"Now you're mine!" Caark snarled.

A small axe whirled past Milo. Caark saw it, but it was

too fast and too late. The blunt side of the axe hit him between the eyes. The headhunter yelled out in pain, tumbled backwards and fell. Milo stared at the unconscious Caark, then searched the trees around the clearing. Standing in a ray of light, he saw his surroundings only as murky shadows.

"You were very lucky," a sonorous voice said behind Milo. He spun around and was stunned once more. If the vile creature had been an incredible sight, this one was all the more so. Right in front of Milo stood, there could be no doubt about it, an elf.

"You are … You're an elf," Milo mumbled, completely in awe. The elf looked at the boy for a long time, seemingly lost in thought.

Milo felt immediately drawn to the tall elf with his pale, weathered and brooding face that was half covered by a gray beard. The elf's black hair, streaked with gray, was long and tied into various braids with leather straps. Another such strap was wrapped around his head, holding the hair down and allowing the ears to proudly point skyward. The elf was lean, muscular and there were scars in his face. He looked as if he had been through countless battles. Where the headhunter was an overall muddy brown, the elf was dressed in shades of dark green, the clothes worn and patched in many places. A thin rope was coiled diagonally across the elf's torso. He carried a small bow on his back and had several arrows in a quiver that seemed stitched into the back of his vest. Different-sized knives were placed in various pockets and sheaths. The elf walked to Caark and inspected his face.

"What happened to his nose?" the elf asked.

"I – I punched him," Milo said.

"You punched Caark?" The elf's eyes seemed to flicker with interest.

Milo nodded. For an instant, the elf just looked at him. Later Milo would tell the others that he thought he saw the forest itself, alive in the tall elf's eyes.

The elf took a small vial from one of the many pockets on his vest, uncorked it and poured the entire content, a bluish powder, into his hand.

"Look at me," the elf said. Milo frowned and did as he was told and before he knew what was happening, the elf blew the powder into the boy's face. As the elf's features blurred, the clearing began to rotate. Milo heard the voice of the elf, loud and clear, as everything around him turned into swirling colors.

"Wychwood is a dangerous place. You will remember neither me nor the attack. You have not been here. You will not come back into the forest. You will never come back into the forest." Milo heard the voice once more, just before he lost consciousness. "About Caark's nose ... Well done."

CHAPTER FOURTEEN

THE OLD KING

He had been revered. A long time ago. He had been loved. He remembered neither place nor time for now but beyond the haze he glimpsed old memories, a time of rounds and colors, a flowing time of … everything.

They had entered the forest now, three younglings of the human kind. Much blood had been spilt in the forest. It had flowed in battle after battle and it had nourished the earth and the trees …

The boy's blood was of a different kind.

The Old King listened, aware now, alive now. Birds nesting above, little ones fighting for food. A badger digging for maggots. An oak he had seen born and grow now lay dead, rotting.

The younglings. They were, somehow, all that mattered.

What had happened? Why was he here? Here in this place they called Wychwood? The younglings were the answer. He had felt a surge of energy in their presence.

He hoped they would come back … and he hoped that Wychwood would not kill them before he was strong enough to reveal himself.

He felt helpless, condemned to wait.

And the Old King frowned.

CHAPTER FIFTEEN

A FATHER'S LOVE

When Milo woke, he was on the garden side of the fence. Corisander sat next to him and was still looking up to the branch where the elf had been moments before. The elf had gently lowered the boy to the ground, then recoiled the rope. With a nod at Corisander, he had disappeared without a sound.

"What – what's …," Milo mumbled, rubbing his eyes.

"We found her," Nick said. Milo spun around to see Nick holding open the fence for Ellie and their mother to step through. Milo jumped up, wobbled and impulsively hugged Lily. "What were you doing?" Nick added. "Sleeping?"

"Let's go inside," Milo said suddenly as he looked at the forest beyond the fence. Nick and Ellie nodded and guided their mother into the house. At the kitchen door, Milo gave Wychwood a final glance and shivered. He waited for Corisander and when the cat was inside, he closed and locked the door. He took up his place on the window sill. The forest lay still and Corisander felt no creatures anywhere near. Milo told them about his encounter with what he described as a bull-like monster version of a dwarf. Milo also told them about the elf, being saved and being powdered. Not once did the others question Milo's story.

A tale about a monster dwarf and a ragged elf might be fantastical in other places of the world. But this was Wychwood and here anything seemed possible.

"He said you won't remember anything," Nick said, frowning.

"Yes," Milo replied.

"But you remember," Nick said.

"I know that," Milo replied, irritated. "It's, all of this is, it's crazy."

"Mom could have died," Ellie whispered.

"… No wonder she never wanted to come back here," Nick muttered.

"We have to leave," Ellie said. "When Dad comes back, we go."

"What do you want to tell him?" Milo asked. "Sorry Dad we don't like it here because there are monsters in the forest that want to eat us and cut our heads off. Is that what you want to tell him?"

"Of course not," Ellie replied, getting upset. "You could have died!"

"Yeah, but you should have seen the elf."

"Ellie's right, Milo," Nick said evenly. "I don't want to die. I don't want any of us to die. We're no Archers, we're Murphys. We're no warriors."

"I am," Milo exclaimed fiercely. "And you are, too. Remember how you threw that knife? Like it or not, we're Archers. We're protectors of Wychwood. Just like that elf."

Nick pensively looked at Milo, then shook his head.

"Oh, come on! The armory? Everything that Grandma told us? And besides, there's Grandma – we can't just come here and leave her alone again. That's why we came here, because she's dying. We have to stay here."

It was obvious to Corisander and the others that Milo, despite the terror that was Caark, had experienced something that he wanted to experience again. Ellie gave Nick a glance and lightly shook her head. She found crayons and paper and began drawing and coloring flowers. Her mother's eyes followed every line the crayons made.

They didn't rise when their father finally came back from the hospital. They heard the car, they heard the front door, they heard him calling and walking to the kitchen. When he saw them all sitting at the table in silence, he assumed that their somber mood was due to their grandmother's collapse.

Corisander looked at him and thought that the man was, in some way, as peculiar as the children. Whatever it was, the sense wasn't as pronounced as it was with the children, but Corisander did sense something. Andrew Murphy was tired, no words, no walls, no pretense. Just a man with his senses laid bare and so the cat felt something deep within. Maybe it had to do with the name – Murphy. Corisander knew all languages, past and present and Murphy, well, Murphy meant "sea warrior".

"It was just her blood pressure," Andrew informed as he pulled up a chair and joined them at the table. "They're running a few more tests but I can go pick her up again tomorrow morning."

"Okay," Ellie muttered.

"Kids, I know this isn't easy for you. But we're here. We're here for Grandma and she's so happy to see you all. I think it really helps her."

"Yeah, me, too. I'm glad we're here. For Grandma," Milo said, looking at Nick and Ellie.

"That's the spirit," Andrew replied. "And you should have seen her at the hospital. The moment she woke up she only talked about you. Wanted to come home again right away but the doctor wouldn't have it. Oh, by the way, did she give you a key?"

"A key?" Ellie asked, startled.

"She didn't give us anything," Nick stated casually. "She just fell unconscious."

"Well," Andrew continued with a shrug, "she was probably still under the influence of whatever they gave her. When she woke up she said something about a key and that you shouldn't use it. Wait for me, she said. Wait for me."

"Weird," Milo said.

Corisander was very rarely discontent and even more rarely envious. He had lived through everything a thousand and one times. But that night, that night Corisander was envious. He saw the love of a father and the warmth of a family and he wished he could belong. To feel that, to be that … Corisander sighed as he watched Andrew pick up their spirits. He rustled up dinner, he made them smile with jokes they had heard a hundred times and through it all the

Irish in him shone strong. When dinner was over, he hummed a ballad and when he ushered them upstairs, he didn't ask them to go to sleep but waved them into the music room instead. Together with Ellie he played a number of melodies, one more mellow and sweet than the one before. Corisander lay down by the open door and watched them all.

Ellie's eyes were closed as she played the flute and swayed with the rhythm of Andrew's tapping left foot. Andrew smiled at the boys while his fingers roamed the buttons of the accordion. Little by little, the boys relaxed and soon Milo clapped and grinned and even Nick began to tap his foot. Andrew just continued tirelessly, intent on raising their spirits, intent on giving his children a good night's sleep and sweet dreams. When Andrew put the accordion away, the children yawned, content and ready to go to sleep. But their father wasn't done yet. When they were in their beds, he asked them all to assemble in the music room once more. Surrounded by books they all took up places on the sofa, the chairs and, in the case of Lily, on the floor. The floral patterns of the rug had her mesmerized. Andrew leaned forward and began to tell the tale of Morraha.

Corisander, stretched out on the sofa next to Ellie, saw the faces of the children light up. Corisander knew the story and guessed that Andrew had told it many times before. Morraha, the story of a man who understood the language of the birds, was turned into a raven, then a horse, then a fox and finally a wolf by his own wife ... and that was just the beginning of the epic tale. Andrew had truly inherited the gift of storytelling. His voice rose and fell with the heartbeats of the tale, he was Morraha, then the wife. He became the animals, even the chicken chased by the fox. The children smiled and laughed and remembered a time when their mother had laughed with them.

As had become customary already, when all went to bed Corisander took up his place at the foot of Milo's bed. Andrew smiled, turned off the light and left the door slightly ajar. Moments later, Nick snuck into Milo's room.

"Just so you know. I've locked the doors downstairs and the keys are hidden in Mom and Dad's bedroom. We should be safe."

Milo nodded.

"I've seen an elf, Nick," Milo said softly.

"Yeah, you told us."

"No, I mean … If there are elves, and monster dwarves … maybe stories like Morraha aren't just stories."

"Let's get some sleep," Nick said.

"We're staying, right?"

"Yeah, we're staying," Nick said and left.

Milo smiled. He looked out beyond the curtains where the dark trees moved in the night and fell into deep slumber that same instant. Corisander stayed awake for a long time, feeling himself the guardian of these children while Roberta Kibble was absent. They didn't stir once and not a single sound disturbed the night. It was as if the love of a father had put a protective spell over the house.

CHAPTER SIXTEEN

THE SAFETY
OF THE TREES

Roberta sat at the kitchen table, her head in her hands. Nick, Milo and Ellie stood on the other side of the table in awkward silence. Roberta tried to stop herself from crying. She could feel hot tears falling into the palm of her hands.

Andrew had picked her up from the hospital right after the doctor's morning visit. She had seen the change in the children's faces the moment she had returned. Retaining her calm, she had done her best to just be there, happy to be alive, happy to be their grandmother, content to be home again. She suggested to Andrew that Lily might enjoy a walk to Oakham Park and Andrew took her up on it without suspicion. And why should he be suspicious? After all, to him, Roberta was just a nice trustworthy old lady living in a charming old house at the edge of a nature preserve.

The moment Andrew and Lily had left the house, she had assembled the children in the kitchen. They seemed relieved to tell her about everything that had happened. Hesitant at first, their voices soon jumbled and jumped each other as they relayed every tiny detail. Roberta had kept her composure until the moment they were all safely out of Wychwood once more. She had just looked at them, staring at them, really. She had been ready to yell at them when she suddenly felt her chest heave. Roberta hadn't cried since the death of her brother and when it hit her, it took her a moment to realize what was happening.

"Well, I guess that's that," she said when she finally lifted her head again. She wiped her eyes and nose with a handkerchief, snorted loudly and sternly looked at them. "Children. Don't ever again enter the forest without my permission."

"We only went because I didn't hold on to Mom," Ellie said, tears welling up as they had when she had told Roberta the first time.

"I understand," Roberta said as she rose. "The only thing that saved you were your instincts as Archers. But instinct alone is not enough. Training begins now." She walked out of the kitchen toward the shed, the children following closely behind her.

"Any more dreams?" she asked casually and was relieved to hear that they had all slept soundly. Roberta saw the cat lounging in the sun on one of Henry Kibble's stones. Corisander raised his head, watched them, then went back to sleep. Roberta knew that the cat wouldn't join them. Corisander didn't seem to like the armory.

"Milo, what you have seen was a redcap. They are a particularly vicious kind of dwarf. Redcaps are headhunters. If you read up on them, you'll see that they dip their caps in the blood of their victims. That they will die unless their caps are soaked with ever more blood.

Utter rubbish, of course. There's nothing mystically magical about these creatures. They're a murderous race and that's all there is to them."

"Redcaps," Milo mused as they entered the shed. "And they're all like Caark?"

"There's just six of them left and yes, they're all like Caark."

Roberta had taken back the key to the armory. She now unlocked the door and led the way down into the chamber below the shed.

"And how many elves are there?" Ellie asked.

"There are five of them, Ellie. Milo, the one you met was their leader, Shendak."

"Shendak," Milo said, more to himself.

"So why are they in Wychwood?" Nick asked.

Roberta turned on the lights in the armory, then checked her watch.

"It's a long story. Basically, Wychwood is their prison," Roberta explained. "Once upon a time there were thousands of them, locked in the forest by a spell. They could not and cannot leave the forest. And so what they have done, ever since the spell was cast, was to battle each other."

"Thousands of them?" Ellie asked with a hush.

Roberta walked across the room to a rack where dozens of dark suits hung in neat rows, organized by sizes. The smallest of the suits seemed made for a young child. They were made of cloth with leather patches protecting chest, wrists, knees and elbows.

"Yes, thousands of them," Roberta echoed back. She looked them up and down, then handed each of them a suit. While they were still frowning and looking at each other, she had already put on her own suit. They stared at her because, as Roberta knew, there was nothing grandmotherly about her now. Her suit, similar to Shendak's, was equipped with sheathed knives, a coiled rope and hooks at her wrists. "Come on, snap to it."

"What are these?" Nick asked, while he struggled to step into his suit.

"Redcaps hunt and kill. They're always on the prowl. What they don't do is climb. That's why we travel in the trees," Roberta explained.

"Huh?" Milo asked.

"We're tree-jumpers, Milo. Same as the elves. Whenever we can, we're up in the safety of the trees. You don't want to end up like Chester," she said and pointed at the headless skeleton that lay on a table against the back wall. She knew she was being harsh, but they needed to really understand. "Whenever possible, you're up in the trees. Clear? All right then, the walk to Oakham Park and back will take them about two hours. Let's make the most of it. Suit up and meet me upstairs."

With that, she climbed up the stairs. They would have many more questions. But there was no time for it now. Roberta held on to the wall when she was at the top of the stairs. She angrily punched the wooden board. Weakness didn't sit well with her, it never had. Archers had never been weak and Roberta had always been the tough one.

Tougher than her father, tougher than her mother, tougher even than her brother. In her youth she had been able to keep up with the elves, with their speed, their accuracy. Roberta shook her head in frustration when she looked at her wrinkled hands. You're still an Archer, she told herself.

When Nick, Milo and Ellie left the shed, their grandmother was nowhere to be seen. Nick pulled at his pants and even the others were clearly ill at ease in their tight-fitting suits. From her hiding place Roberta smiled. They'd get used to the outfits soon enough.

"Well, what are you waiting for?" Roberta said from high up, hidden behind the foliage of an oak tree. The children looked around.

"I don't like playing games," Nick quietly mouthed.

"This is no game," Roberta said, stepping out on one of the branches. They all gaped up at her. "You are protectors of Wychwood, Children. You will save lives and you will put your own in danger. No, this is no game." Then she smiled. "But it is more wonderful than anything else in this world."

"Grandma, watch out!" Nick called up as she ran along a sturdy branch toward the outer end of it, then jumped and bounced up, as if jumping off a diving board into a pool. The branch propelled her upwards, where she did a turn in mid-air, away from the upper branch that could have saved her. Ellie gasped, certain that Roberta would fall.

Nick and Milo ran forward, racing to get there in time to catch her. But Roberta didn't come crashing down through the branches of the tree. She was dangling from the branch she had been sure to miss. To their astonishment, she wasn't holding on. She was hanging by the hooks that were sown into the sleeves of her suit jacket.

"Oh my, I haven't done this in a while," Roberta said, smiling and breathing heavily. "These hooks have saved me a thousand times over." She swung to the side, took hold of another branch and sat down. "Are you coming?"

"How did you get up there?" Ellie asked.

"Rope," Roberta said. "But you'll start with the basics. Climb."

"The tree's on the other side of the fence, Grandma," Nick said.

"Yes, it is," she replied. "You'll be fine."

"You just told us to always be up in the trees," Nick insisted.

"You're under the protection of your grandmother," she replied.

Milo didn't go back to the opening in the fence, he climbed over it. Fast as squirrel, he was on the other side.

"Come on, guys. If Grandma says it's fine, it's fine."

Nick and Ellie reluctantly followed. As she waited for them, Roberta had two knives at the ready. The redcaps could appear anywhere, anytime. They not only knew the forest inside out, they had also built tunnels and halls below ground. Roberta put the knives away when the children sat down next to her. She looked from one to the other. While there were degrees of hesitation, there was no fear.

"Archers, indeed," Roberta said with a smile.

"What now?" Milo said eagerly.

"Now we begin," Roberta said.

She told them about the different kinds of trees, about branches and bark. She explained which wood would bend and which would snap. She impressed constant alertness on them, eyes ahead, focused on the next steps, the next grips. One wrong move could mean a painful fall … or worse. When Roberta explained how the trees reacted differently with the seasons, she saw them getting restless. Milo was standing already, looking at the trees around them, planning his first move, his second and third.

"Remember what I told you. Keep your eyes open. The leather will protect you from cuts and scrapes. Cling to the tree, slide down, try branches, swing on the light ones, use the hooks and, most important, trust your instinct. Now go, Archers, go!"

Milo was off before the others even got to their feet. Planned and executed perfectly, he jumped, spun, hung on the wrist hooks for a moment, then spun again to land on the branch below. Nick frowned, watching Milo take another leap. He was just about to ask Ellie to be cautious when she jumped past him.

If Milo had moved swiftly and elegantly, it was nothing compared to Ellie. She jumped, swung, whirled, spun and ran with pure grace. She came to land next to Milo with a beautifully executed somersault.

"Show off," Milo said gruffly and yet it was obvious that he was not just impressed but also proud of his sister's performance.

"Your turn, Nick!" she called, her face glowing with excitement.

"Shut up," Nick hissed. "They're down there somewhere."

"He's right, Ellie," Roberta called over to their tree. "They won't climb trees but they're deadly with their pikes."

"They throw them?" Nick asked quietly.

"Throw, hook, stab, slice, ram … you name it, Nick. The pike's a fearsome weapon," Roberta said. "Now off you go."

"I'm heavier than they are," Nick said grudgingly.

"Yes, you are," Roberta said with a grin. "Their moves are not yours. Find your own. Look at the trees, look closely and you'll see your path. Now go."

Nick took a step back, inhaled, exhaled and Roberta saw it going wrong before he jumped off the branch. A step too late, the branch sagged and slipped away sideways under Nick's foot. He managed to grab hold of the branch as he fell, swung and slammed against the trunk of the beech. He slid down the trunk, scrambling to grab hold of something. Roberta saw the fear in his eyes, saw him looking down. Nick would have to learn to get out of his head, she thought. And learn he would, one way or another.

Roberta was about to jump toward him when he was stopped by a branch. Fear changed to frustration and anger as he clambered up the tree, then jumped across to where

Milo and Ellie stood waiting for him.

"I hate this crap," Nick murmured under his breath.

"The old woman has excellent hearing, Nick," Roberta divulged.

"You'll get it," Ellie said encouragingly.

"You're right, Ellie," Milo smirked, barely able to control the grin that was spreading across his face. "The way he hugged that tree was just … beautiful."

When Nick smacked Milo against the back of his head, Milo burst out laughing. Just as Roberta arrived next to them, Milo jumped off again, still roaring with laughter.

"Don't worry, Nick," Roberta said.

"I'm not worried," Nick replied, clearly annoyed as he picked leaves and twigs from his suit.

"Good," Roberta said, ignoring his attitude. "By this evening, you'll feel as if you'd been tree-jumping your whole life."

Nick didn't reply. He did his best to remain calm when Ellie gave him an encouraging smile and a pat on the back before jumping off, effortlessly, after Milo.

"She's something," Roberta said.

Nick rolled his eyes and ran after Ellie. This time he picked a better path. He stumbled and slipped once, but instantly recovered and moved on. Roberta liked what she saw.

Basic tree-jumping training continued that way for the following three days. Roberta would find something to do for Andrew and Lily. Sometimes she would send them on errands, sometimes for special walks. Andrew, hesitant at first, soon enjoyed the trips with Lily, especially as he saw how happy the children were in the company of their grandmother. They seemed energized, the fresh country air clearly agreed with them.

Roberta pushed them, every day a little more. As she had promised Nick, he soon kept pace with the others. Because of his weight, he picked different branches, ran faster and jumped further, evading the lighter branches Ellie was able to use. For three days, they jumped the high trees along the fence, never going deeper into Wychwood ... and for three days she occasionally, casually, enquired about their dreams. Roberta was relieved to hear that they had experienced no more dreams since their first night in the company of the forest.

Once in a while Roberta felt that they were being watched and the children felt it, too. Maybe it was the redcaps, maybe it was the elves, they never saw anyone. Roberta noticed that the animals of the forest were moving about in odd ways. She had seen a deer ramming a tree, then blankly staring at the trunk. Half a half dozen woodpeckers chasing each other around an oak tree again and again. And just yesterday she had seen a hare chasing a fox. Something was happening but it was nothing that made sense to Roberta. Just stay alert, she told herself.

Roberta checked her watch. It was time. She had sent Andrew to Oxford for a special medicine that couldn't be found anywhere else. A lie, of course. But it meant a nice visit to Oxford for Andrew and Lily – and extended training time for the children. Roberta gave off a high-pitched whistle, the call for them to return.

She couldn't see them but she heard them coming through the foliage. Ellie gracefully landed next to Roberta, her face flushed. Moments later Milo and Nick followed. All of them were sweating and breathing heavily – and all of them glowed.

"Any falls?" Roberta asked.

"No falls, no scrapes, no bruises," Milo said.

"All good," Nick agreed. Roberta saw that there were scrapes on his face and twigs stuck in his suit. He was getting there.

"All right then. Tomorrow we'll start swinging," Roberta said. She uncoiled the rope around her shoulder and threw the grapnel hook that was attached to one end around one of the high branches. With a light bounce she launched herself into the air, swung down and smoothly landed next to the shed. As she recoiled the rope, she watched them with pride. Squirrel-like, they jumped from branch to branch, lower and lower and all used their own paths. Ellie ran out an ever more bending branch, then hung on to its end by one hand. It delivered her softly to the grass. The branch whipped back in place as the boys jumped the last bit. While Milo rolled then stood, Nick landed on his two feet and stood, planted like a tree.

"Clean up," Roberta said and walked away into the shed.

CHAPTER SEVENTEEN

TWELVE
THOUSAND STRONG

The warmth in the kitchen had little to do with temperature. Corisander knew that it was the sum of everything, the spices and the leaves, the heartbeats, the pulsing blood, the spider in the corner, the clanging of the pots and the vibrations of the voices.

While Roberta had prepared dinner, Lily had wandered, accompanied by Milo and Corisander, through the garden. Lily had occasionally glanced at the forest but had stayed away from it. Instead she walked through the flower and spice patches. Her hands caressed the plants and here and there she picked a flower, picked a leaf. As they sat at dinner later, the table was decorated with the things Lily had picked.

"Has she done this before?" Roberta asked.

"Yes," Andrew replied, patting Lily's hand. "She has this affinity for plants. Even in New York, we go for walks in the park every day."

"She likes drawing," Ellie said. "Flowers and circles, mostly. And she decorates, too."

"She doesn't decorate," Milo said. "She just leaves things."

Corisander felt the boy's sadness beneath the words. They all still remembered being embraced by their mother, playing with her, laughing with her. But those memories were fading. For years now they had lived with a mist of a mother, something to be barely seen, barely felt, barely there. The cat wondered about Lily and not for the first time. No incident had brought on her condition. She had simply retreated and when Corisander felt into her, he only felt distant swirls of the flow. Lying on the window sill, Corisander chided himself. He had just tried to make sense of things. How utterly unnecessary. How utterly human. And yet his curiosity rose again when Lily started humming.

"How about this?" Roberta asked. "Has she done this before?"

Andrew and the children stared at Lily. It was clear that she hadn't hummed before. Andrew lightly shook his head and no one spoke. Something was happening and Corisander saw Ellie holding her breath so as not to disturb it. The melody Lily hummed was one Andrew had played on his accordion. He very gently added his own hum to Lily's. For a moment, Lily stopped, a frown on her face as if she had heard something far away. Then she began again and hummed in tune with Andrew. Ellie joined in, no more than a whisper. She exchanged glances with her father and he smiled at her, then nodded at the boys. First Nick, then Milo joined in humming the melody, then Roberta joined in, too.

Corisander had never heard a more beautiful sound. It

was a moment human beings called magical when all it really meant was that the world was flowing freely in that moment. They continued humming, interrupted only by quick bites and gulps. They smiled when they did the dishes and the humming continued.

"I'm so happy I could burst," Andrew whispered to Roberta. "It's this place. And you. Thank you so much for bringing us here, Roberta." He gave her an impulsive hug, then continued humming, now following Lily's lead.

Lily still sat at the table, looking at the flowers and leaves still there, looking at the plates as they were carried away. She hummed and continued humming and then she looked up, straight at Andrew, and smiled.

Corisander could hear the man's heart skipping a beat.

"Lily?" he said in a hush.

She continued looking at him, smiling.

"Mom?" Milo said, touching her arm.

When Andrew moved, her eyes stayed focused on the spot he had just vacated. Lily kept on smiling at the wall. Still, the man wasn't discouraged. He took Lily by the hand and she rose without hesitation.

"I'll play her a few more melodies," he said. "Lily, let's go upstairs. Kids, are you coming, too?"

"We'll join you when we're done here," Roberta said.

Andrew nodded, beamed at them all and joined in the melody of Lily's hum again as he led her out of the room and up the stairs. The moment he was gone, Roberta put away the kitchen towel and sat down.

"Wychwood seems to agree with her," Roberta said.

"It's wonderful," Ellie said.

"You never told us why she left," Milo said.

"And why she never wanted to come back," Nick added.

Ellie and Milo joined Roberta at the table. Nick leaned against the wall by the window, his fingers lazily stroking Corisander's back. Corisander purred.

"Let me explain the dome," Roberta began with a heavy sigh. "It was created three thousand years ago, when humans reached out and took hold everywhere. You must know that before our time the world was a very different one. The world was, you might say, a richer one, one that was filled with imagination beyond anything we know today. Before humanity made its appearance on the planet, the world was one of creatures of every kind, you might call them magical. At that time, the flow was still strong."

"Huh? What?" Milo asked.

"What's the flow?" Nick asked.

"The flow is what created the Earth, Nick. Call it matter, call it energy ... or call it magic, I will leave that up to you. Just understand that, in the beginning, the Earth was flowing. The flow was not a thing, it was everything and everyone."

"Everyone?" Ellie asked.

"Spirits, entities, beings," Roberta said. "The flow was filled with them, was made of them, was them. They were just there and they played, for eons in a world that would have looked like a giant ball of lava to our eyes. There was no good and there was no evil, no up and no down, no constant in the ever-changing flow ... and when the planet

109

finally took its form, the flow found its way into the fairy creatures."

"You're saying there were elves and dwarves when there were dinosaurs?" Nick asked and his expression clearly conveyed what he thought of the idea.

"Indeed," Roberta said and grinned. "I realize how all of this must sound to you. But do bear with me. Yes, there were elves and dwarves, and giants, and sprites, and dragons and fairy creatures of every kind. The flow was still coursing through a world far more vibrant than the one we know today. In fact, many of the creatures back then were flowen."

"What does that mean?" Ellie asked.

"You would call them shapeshifters," Roberta explained. "Beings with the ability to change form as they pleased. They had the flow within them."

"There really were shapeshifters?" Milo asked. He was deeply frowning as he listened to Roberta, trying to take in what she knew had to sound crazy to them.

"Just as there really were giants and dragons," Roberta said with a nod. "For thousands of years we've been telling the stories of a time when all of those creatures were real. You see, there was a time when their kind and ours shared the planet in peace."

"What does any of this have to do with the dome?" Nick asked impatiently.

"We are a noisy bunch, Nick," Roberta explained. "And an industrious bunch. We cut down the trees, we tilled the fields and we took up more room, always more. Human endeavors began to reach into every corner of the world. With the growing population, the forests were cleared to give way to farms and fields. The noise humans brought was unbearable for fairy beings and it forced them to retreat further and further."

Roberta paused. While talking, she had made tea and now handed them each a steaming cup. She was telling it well, Corisander thought. Hard to believe any of it, of course. But then in the past few days the children had already experienced a great deal they had never even considered before. From upstairs the accordion filled the air with gentle tunes. Roberta took a sip of her tea, set it down and continued.

"Three thousand years ago, right here in this very spot, the fairy creatures had enough."

"What happened?" Nick asked.

"They couldn't stand the noise any longer, the hammering, the sawing and the hacking. There were those who fled into the quiet places of the world. There were those who took on forms in order to survive. And there were those who were unwilling to change and unwilling to give way – and so the hunting and the killing began. … Three thousand years ago, those who remained decided to take a stand. Beings of every kind assembled in the forest of Arn."

"Arn is Wychwood?" Milo asked.

"Yes, the tiny little bit that's left of what was once a vast forest. There were giants and spirits, elves and dwarves, fairies big and small. It was what they felt was their last

111

stand. It was to give up and disappear – or to stand and fight. It was an army of twelve thousand to eradicate humanity, to kill every man, woman and child."

"But that never happened," Ellie said, wanting Roberta to go on.

"Obviously," Nick said.

"It could have gone the other way, Nick. Those twelve thousand could have wiped humanity off the face of the Earth. Before the battle, two powerful sages, you would call them wizards today, found themselves on opposite sides. Andill argued for peace, Ardunn for battle. Andill believed that their time had come to its natural end. In his belief, the creatures had to evolve and become part of the world shaped by humans. What Andill believed was something that Ardunn could not accept. When his battle cry pitched twelve thousand creatures into a frenzy, Andill spoke words that could not be heard. The spell grew from those words and it kept on growing until it stretched over all of Arn. With that one moment, the forest had become a prison. No creature would be able to cross the threshold. They were doomed to live forever in each other's company."

"They are immortal?" Nick asked.

"They are indeed," Roberta replied with a light nod. "The few alive today have been there at the time before the dome."

"Shendak and Caark are three thousand years old?" Milo asked in disbelief.

"Older than that, Milo."

"But they can be killed," Nick said.

"Yes," Roberta said. "Imagine, twelve thousand creatures, giants among them and dragons … and all that's left today are five elves and six dwarves. When the spell was first cast, they tried everything to undo its power. For hundreds of years they tried every spell and every attack. The dome held and still holds today. The green prison drove many of them mad – and then it got worse. You see, humanity didn't suddenly stop growing. They kept expanding, needing more room, needing more wood and so Arn was cut down more and more and with it the prison contracted. The old name forgotten, it became Wychwood and within the shrinking forest, ever fewer creatures remained. Some took their own lives and some turned into monsters. Redcaps haven't always been as they are today."

"What about that retired cop?" Nick asked.

"Christopher Smith," Ellie added.

"A good man," Roberta said.

"He said hundreds of people have gone missing," Nick said.

"And that's true – hunted down and killed by redcaps," Roberta said matter-of-factly.

"I thought you were protecting the forest and all those within," Ellie said.

Roberta leaned forward. Her voice was deep and dark when she continued.

"Both elves and Archers have given their lives to save the innocents. But we cannot be everywhere all the time. Sometimes a wanderer gets lost in the forest, sometimes a tourist or a poacher. Most often we find them before the caps do. We wipe their memories and send them on their way. What do you think would happen if I told the police about everything I've just told you?

"They would think you're crazy," Nick said.

"Exactly. Since I became a tree-jumper, we've lost only sixteen people to the dwarves. Sixteen – in almost seventy years. You know how many we saved in my time? And these are just the ones I know of – we've saved over two thousand people. Lord Thornton is one of the few who knows, which is why there's a fence around Wychwood. I'll introduce you. We'll be visiting Oakham Park House on Monday."

"We'll meet a lord?" Ellie asked.

"He is a regular person, Ellie, just like you and me except that he's rich and lives in a palace because one of his ancestors helped Sir Francis Drake defeat the Spanish Armada. Good story but one for another time."

"You still haven't told us why Mom never wanted to come back here," Nick said.

Roberta sighed. Whether it was her age, the cancer, the training or thinking about that day such a long time ago, she felt infinitely tired.

"... You've seen the skeleton in the armory?" she asked.

The children nodded uncomfortably.

"I'm sure you've guessed that it's my brother Chester ... most of him. His skull is in the redcaps' trophy hall. The head of an Archer ... lined up in a row with the skulls of thousands of others, giants, fairies, elves. They never got

114

an Archer until they got Chester."

Roberta rose and walked to the door.

"It was a bad day … and your mother saw it all. That's why she left and that's why she never wanted you to come here. Get a good night's rest, children."

They listened to Roberta's heavy steps as she climbed the stairs. The children just sat there, looking at the surface of the old table before them. Corisander jumped off the window sill and up onto the table. He flopped down and, stretching, rolled onto his back. This sort of behavior usually lifted the spirit of humans and it was no different now. Ellie smiled and Nick rubbed the cat's belly and eventually Milo smiled, too. Upstairs, Andrew was still playing the accordion and Lily was still humming.

"Well, we asked," Nick said evenly.

"She totally went epic on us," Milo said. "The story is … unreal."

"Not story … history," Nick said.

"Maybe you were a fairy once," Ellie said to Corisander while scratching him below the chin. Corisander stopped purring and looked at her.

"Meow," Corisander replied. I wish I could tell you more, Corisander thought.

Spirits lifted, Corisander walked with the children. Nick locked the doors and put away the keys as he did every night now. Their dreams and Milo's sleepwalking that first night seemed ancient history, but what they had seen and heard these past days was enough reason for caution.

Corisander watched them brush their teeth and say

goodnight to their parents. Lily lay flat on the carpet, eyes closed and humming while Andrew just kept on playing one sweet melody after another.

When they were all asleep, Corisander jumped from Milo's bed and hopped up onto the window sill. He gazed up at the stars and then into the forest. Wychwood lay peaceful, quiet. The days had been sunny, the weather lazily remaining the same. On the surface, there was complete calm. But Corisander sensed a tension in the forest. The animals inside Wychwood were uneasy in their sleep. Corisander sighed. Roberta would continue to train her grandchildren and, with every new day, she would put them in greater danger. She wouldn't rest until her brother's skull was reunited with the rest of his skeleton.

And while they seemed to have forgotten about the spirit that had reached out for them, Corisander had not.

Who are you, Corisander thought.

Wychwood didn't move and yet, something, some thing, seemed to be there.

CHAPTER EIGHTEEN

THE OLD KING

Day after day the old woman had come back into Wychwood, bringing the younglings. They had roamed from tree to tree and their presence had made the Old King giddy. He didn't remember smiling. He didn't know if he could. But it felt like smiling. That feeling as, day after day, he grew stronger because of them.

He remembered Andill and Ardunn now – and he remembered how simple it had been to take a side. The clamor of humanity had driven the Old King mad. Wychwood was quiet. Maybe this was best. Maybe the Old King should go back to nothingness.

He felt the trees move and he longed for the younglings to return. He saw the birds take flight and the deer raise their heads and look for something unseen. He was being felt again. He was far from the spirit he had once been, but he was here once more and he was growing, slowly, steadily, patiently.

And the Old King smiled.

CHAPTER NINETEEN

INTO THE FOREST

Roberta had been up early, preparing the day. Tea in flasks, pouches filled with tightly wrapped sandwiches and a check-through of her first aid kit. She had used that kit more times than she cared to remember.

She just finished packing her bag when Andrew walked into the kitchen, rubbing his eyes.

"Morning, Roberta. Where are the kids?"

"They told me that they wanted to go explore Finstock," Roberta replied.

"That's a first," Andrew said, shaking his head. "It's not even seven o'clock and they're out in the actual fresh air? Nuts."

"Coffee's ready," Roberta said, pointing at the filled pot. "Lily's still asleep?"

"Yes, yes she is," Andrew said with a smile. He poured himself a large cup, sipped carefully and smiled even more broadly. "Yesterday was magical. I must have played for her way past midnight and she hummed along with every tune. Something's happening, Roberta. I'm so glad we came here."

"Wychwood is a wondrous place," Roberta said as she had said many times before. "Well, you enjoy your day with Lily, Andrew," she added. "I'm off to meet a friend of mine and if I see the children, I'll show them some more of the sights."

"What sights are you talking about? Oakham Park is certainly impressive but other than that? What else is there to see around here?"

"Ah, dear Andrew, I find the sights of nature ever so much more impressive. I might show them the walks along the River Evenlode. Or explore the hills around Wychwood. You know, legends have it that giants are buried beneath those hills."

"Tales of Wychwood," Andrew said and smiled at her. "Please take care of yourself, Roberta. If you get tired, you just call my cellular and I'll pick you up."

"I've never had one of those mobile phones and never will. They hurt my ears even when they're not ringing and they hardly ever work around here anyway. Don't you worry about me. Any problems, the good people of Finstock will be glad to assist."

With that, Roberta put on her coat and left the house. Andrew waved at her from the upstairs music room as she walked out onto Witney Road. She continued on past the tall hedges, then snuck back into the property, walked around the house and disappeared in the shed. There, waiting for her, suited up and ready to go, were the children.

"Big day ahead," Roberta stated as she put on her tree-jumper suit.

"Awesome," Milo replied.

Milo was high-fiving Ellie as Roberta gave them all coiled

ropes with grapnel hooks. She explained how to hook them into their belts, how to shoot and retract them.

"This may sound easy but I can assure you it'll take a while until you get the hang of it. As long as you can jump from tree to tree, you jump. When you need additional speed, or have to cross a wider distance to reach a next tree, you use the ropes. There are a hundred different ways to swing, depending on the circumstance. Today we'll look at some of them."

Roberta turned to the rack that held her weapons. She sheathed several knives and her favorite hatchet.

"We might need weapons, too," Milo suggested eagerly.

"You worry about staying in the trees, young man, I worry about the rest," Roberta said, walking to the stairs. She looked at the children and saw that Nick was brooding. "What is it, Nick?"

"Why are we doing this?" Nick asked.

"Dude, we're protectors of Wychwood," Milo replied.

"We are Nick, Milo and Eliza Murphy of New York City, here to visit our grandmother. That's who we are. Why show us all this stuff, Grandma?"

"Because we're also Archers, Nick," Ellie offered.

"That's not what I mean," Nick replied, annoyed. "Soon we'll be flying back to our lives on the other side of the Atlantic. What's the point to all of this then?"

"You're right," Roberta said and meant it. Of course Nick was right. Of course her entire plan was ludicrous. It didn't make sense but then again, she had learned a long time ago that not everything needed to make sense. "I just … I just didn't want all of this to be over. That's all. I wanted you to know about the life of an Archer, what we did, what we meant, who we really were for the past three hundred years. With my death, the armory and everything that has ever been would have been forgotten. Now you know … and maybe that's all that I had a right to hope for. We can take off the suits, lock up the armory and go play bridge … if that's what you want."

"I want us to not die," Nick said.

"Oh, come on, Nick!" Milo said, increasingly annoyed.

"Ellie?" Nick asked. She looked from Nick to Milo.

"We'll be careful," Ellie replied.

"And we can stop anytime," Roberta said.

"All right?" Milo asked Nick.

Finally, Nick nodded.

"Heck," Nick said, "I mean what can happen, right?"

Milo grinned and tried to high-five and fist-bump Nick. Nick just rolled his eyes and walked past him up the stairs.

Moments later they were jumping and swinging from tree to tree. Roberta was amazed to see just how quickly the children learned to execute the right moves. For the first time they jumped away from the edge of the forest, straight toward the middle of Wychwood. It was there where the trees were higher, where Wychwood had remained untouched and wild.

Nick was flawless in the way he used the ropes. He was first in shooting the grapnel hook and swinging off. No hesitation, pure focus. He landed on an alder tree three seconds later, casually walking to the trunk while retracting the rope. As they continued, Roberta noticed that Nick's earlier concerns were replaced by the joy of flying through the air. When he thought that no one could see it, he was grinning.

"We're heading to Newhill Plain. It's a large clearing in the middle of Wychwood," Roberta explained, before jumping off again. She knew the children to be behind her. She heard their ropes fly out and retract. Branches creaked, trunks bent and leaves rustled. As they made their way toward the center of the forest, they saw footpaths, narrow brooks and glittering ponds far below. As they progressed, Roberta was only too aware that the children were pacing themselves. They would appear to the left and right of Roberta, then wait and fall behind again. Old age and impending death don't go well with tree-jumping, Roberta thought and heard herself give off a low growl. By the time Roberta reached the top of a beech on the edge of Newhill Plain, she was exhausted. Breathing heavily, she coiled her rope as the others arrived next to her.

"Best day ever," Milo said.

"Yup," Ellie said, beaming as she gazed across the tree tops.

"Yeah, not bad," Nick said and jumped out of the way before Milo could punch him.

"Are you okay, Grandma?" Ellie asked, a frown on her face.

"All things considered, yes," Roberta replied and put on a smile. She would ignore the pain. One more time. Quickly changing topic, she pointed at the vast clearing below. "That's Newhill Plain. The opening over there is called Grand Vista, an alley through the trees that leads straight to Oakham Park House."

Roberta sat down, leaned against the trunk of the beech and signaled the children to do the same. When they had been sitting in silence for a while, Roberta spoke again.

"Do you sense anything?"

"Nice breeze," Nick said. "But I guess that's not what you mean."

"Close your eyes," Roberta said. One by one they followed her request. "Now listen. Listen around you. Listen up, down, in every direction. Listen. There are deer, walking there to the right of us."

Ellie and Nick opened their eyes but couldn't see the deer. Roberta asked them to close their eyes once more.

"It's not sight, it's sensation. Sometimes, if we just allow ourselves to flow with the motion of the trees around us, we can sense a great deal. Right now, I sense the deer. And there's a fox nearby –"

"Hunting a bird, a big bird. I think a pheasant." When Milo opened his eyes, he saw that all were looking at him. "And the deer – there were three of them, right? And there's an owl in that tree over there."

"That's quite impressive, young man," Roberta said, smiling.

"How's that work?" Nick asked.

"I don't know," Milo said with a shrug. "It sort of feels like heat. Like if you pay attention, you can tell what's there and what shape it is."

"Most of the Archers have had this sense, some less, some more," Roberta explained. "It can help a –"

"Someone's coming," Milo said in a hush.

Roberta put her fingers to her lips. Through the foliage they caught glimpses of three redcaps and Roberta knew from the look on Milo's face that he recognized Caark among them. From this high up, it was difficult to see what exactly they were up to. Still, Roberta knew their ways. Whenever redcaps were above ground they were mostly silent. They hunted in packs. Right at that moment, they sniffed the air.

Roberta sent the children an assuring glance to indicate that they were safe. She could see their agitation but, where Nick and Ellie were nervous, Milo seemed to be more angry than anything else. Just don't move, Roberta thought. As long as the children remained motionless, the dwarves wouldn't discover their presence. Roberta felt the light wind in her face. Good. It meant their scent was blowing away across Newhill Plain.

When the redcaps huddled close to the trunk of their tree and squatted down, Roberta sighed. The dwarves stopped moving, as if they had suddenly turned to stone. They often sat that way for hours, sometimes for days. After all, they did have all the time in the world. Roberta looked at the sun. It was the middle of the day.

Six hours later they were still in the exact same spot. Nick had found himself a comfortable place, moving there, inch by inch, over the course of half an hour. Ellie occasionally moved her arms and legs, ever so slowly, to keep the blood circulating. Milo hadn't moved as he kept on staring down at Caark. Roberta was most worried about him doing something stupid. The sun was sinking to the west of Newhill Plain, but they'd still have daylight until past nine o'clock.

Roberta could barely feel her legs. She was beginning to think about a distraction plan that would greatly endanger the children – when the dwarves finally moved. It happened in a flash. A large boar wandered, grunting, searching the ground with its snout, too close to the three redcaps. Immobile as they sat in the shadows of the tree and with the wind taking their scent away from the animal, the boar had no chance.

The children were shocked when they saw the redcaps jump into sudden action. From their squatting position they pounced forward, pulled their knives and axes in mid-air and slew the boar. Satisfied with their kill, they smeared themselves with the blood of the animal, then hacked it into two parts. Caark pushed and kicked his companions until they shouldered a boar half each and walked off.

Roberta waited another five minutes before she spoke.

"Let's go," she said, laboriously getting to her feet.

"That was horrible," Ellie said with a shudder.

"That was Caark," Milo said.

While the others stood and readied to go, Nick still sat, deep in thought.

"Care to join us?" Roberta asked.

"Why not just kill them?" he asked, looking up at her. "These are vicious creatures who have caused nothing but death and misery. Why haven't the elves and the Archers just gone ahead and killed them all?"

"First," Roberta began, "redcaps are fierce and powerful. You can't just kill a redcap. Second, we're not killers, Nick. We are protectors."

"But you wouldn't have to protect Wychwood anymore if there were no more redcaps," Nick insisted. "All of this would be over. You have killed dwarves, right?"

"I have killed seven of them," Roberta replied grimly. "I have killed seven immortal beings from a time before our time and I am not proud of what I have done. I have killed them in combat, one on one, when it was either my life or theirs. They know no mercy. We do. The elves do. Those vicious creatures, as you call them, have slain many. So have lions and wolves and foxes and bears and eagles and owls … would you kill them all? They are predators, we are not. We are protectors of the forest and of those who roam within. That is what it means to be an Archer."

Nick stared at her and gave a light nod as he rose. Milo looked from Roberta to Nick and when he thought the argument over, he jumped before Roberta could point out the direction. The boy knew instinctively. Ellie followed her brother a second later and Roberta saw her swinging past Milo. Before Nick jumped, Roberta took his arm.

"Nick, your argument is a valid one. Archers have had that same argument time and time again over the centuries. But in the end, we have always believed that we should aspire to be better than them."

"Are you?" Nick asked.

"… I am trying to be," Roberta said.

Nick nodded and jumped off.

Roberta took another look at the darkening forest. She had always loved the view from this place. She hoped that Nick would never know what killing felt like. It would change him forever.

Roberta flexed her old muscles, strained her eyes to make sense of the path before her … and jumped.

CHAPTER TWENTY

THE DOCTOR
OF WYCHWOOD

As the sun set and the shadows deepened, Roberta saw that it was becoming more difficult for the children to pick their paths.

They moved in silence and became more cautious with every darkening minute. Caution could be a good thing, Roberta knew, but it could also be dangerous. When it came to tree-jumping, caution brought reason into the equation and pushed instinct aside. Still, they moved forward steadily and in a direct line toward the house.

Roberta felt every muscle, every sinew, every bone. She had prepared herself for this one last day in the trees with every healing and strengthening potion she had been able to think of. But no potion could remove the weakness she felt at that moment. The children waited for her two trees ahead. She held on to the trunk of the ash she was standing on. She breathed heavily, tried to connect herself to the swaying of the tree.

Roberta hated the fact that death was winning, that she couldn't fight that opponent, that she couldn't take her hatchet into that one last battle for an even chance.

She flung the rope and jumped – just as a spooked flock

of pigeons crossed her path. Hit by bird wings, the rope shuddered and Roberta knew that the grapnel hook would miss its mark. I'm going to fall, she thought. She tried to throw another rope, something that might have worked in her youth. Roberta went crashing through the foliage, felt intense pain as her head whipped against a thick branch, spiraled and hit two more branches before slamming into the mossy forest floor.

In a flash, Nick, Milo and Ellie were next to her.

"Into the trees," Roberta said, forcing every word from her mouth. "Now!"

She could barely see and she couldn't move her head. Ellie knelt beside her, eyes wide with fear. She held Roberta's head and saw the blood on her hands. Milo picked up a branch and scanned the surroundings.

"We're getting you up into the tree, Grandma," Nick said.

"I can take care of — myself," she said and lost consciousness.

"Milo, help me," Nick whispered urgently.

As they bent down to lift her, Milo stopped.

"Quiet," he whispered.

"Shit," Nick hissed and the panic he felt was in the eyes of the others, too. Instinctively, he took his grandmother's hatchet, while Milo took two of her big knives and handed the smaller one to Ellie. They stood in silence. They heard nothing. Nick, frustrated, looked at Milo and gestured, "Well? Anything?"

Then he heard it, too. Something was crashing through

the underbrush nearby and the sounds were coming closer fast.

"Ellie, get up in the tree," Nick shouted.

"I'm not leaving Grandma," she shot back at him.

"We're getting her," Milo said. "Get up there!"

Nick forcefully grabbed Ellie, trying to push her up into the lowest branches. She pushed against him as he lifted her, ran up the tree trunk and flipped over her brother's head with an effortless summersault. Nick turned to see her staring at him.

"I said I'm not leaving Grandma."

Whatever was coming, was coming fast and so they all stood before their grandmother, weapons raised, shielding her. Fear pushed aside, they were breathing deeply and stood, ready to attack, feet solidly planted.

"This sucks," Nick hissed.

"We can take them," Milo shot back.

"You're crazy," Nick replied.

"Archers," Milo said and it was like a call to arms.

"Archers," Nick and Ellie echoed.

The hazel and elder bushes split apart to reveal an old man, skinny and wearing what looked like a monk's robe, a pouch over his shoulder and carrying a long staff. The Archers looked at each other in confusion.

The old man stopped for just a moment. He frowned at them, lightly shaking his head, then spotting Roberta behind them.

"Roberta," he called out. Completely ignoring the weapons pointed at him, he rushed past them to kneel next

130

to Roberta. Nick tried to yank the old man away from her but he pulled free. "She needs my help."

The children frowned at each other, helpless, wondering. But as it did appear that the strange old man was sincere in his efforts, they just stood and watched as he examined Roberta's arms and legs.

"Who are you?" Nick asked.

"There is blood at the back of her head," Ellie said and showed her bloodied hand.

Instantly, the old man felt Roberta's head and neck. He nodded to himself and hurriedly took a small jar from the pouch he carried over his shoulder. When he opened it, they all took a step back, the stench was overpowering.

"What is that?" Milo asked.

"The thing that will save your grandmother's life," the old man said. Without hesitation, he took the content of the jar and rubbed the brown goo onto the back of Roberta's neck. He then began to bandage her head with an old piece of cloth. As he did, he seemed to relax. "You are her grandchildren, aren't you?"

"Yes," Ellie said.

"Who are you?" Nick asked again.

"Ashford Bromley," the old man said. Roberta's head bandaged, he now propped her up against the tree. Bromley pushed an acorn-sized dark brown ball into her mouth and made sure she swallowed. Then he sighed and rose. "She'll be fine."

"We have to get her up into the tree," Milo said.

"No need to worry. There aren't any redcaps anywhere

near right now," Bromley said.

"You know about the redcaps?" Ellie asked.

"I know everything about the forest," he replied. "Lived here all my life. I'm surprised Roberta hasn't told you about me," he added.

"How do you know that there are no redcaps?" Milo asked

"I just know," Bromley said. "Still, you should get going."

"How are we going to get Grandma back?" Ellie asked.

"Oh, she's quite all right," Bromley said and lightly kicked the sole of her shoe. To the surprise of the children, Roberta opened her eyes immediately. She rose, completely disorientated and shaky on her feet. She noticed Bromley and smiled.

"Ashford," she said, "how nice to see you." When the scent of Bromley's healing goo reached her nose, she shook her head in disgust.

"What do you want? It works," he proclaimed with a grin.

"I see you've met my grandchildren. Ellie, Milo, Nick, this is Ashford Bromley, the doctor of Wychwood."

"At your service," Bromley said with a light bow. "Roberta, may I talk to you for a moment?"

Roberta nodded and walked with him out of hearing distance. She saw that the children were watching them. She noticed that the kids were carrying her weapons. The hatchet looked good in Nick's hands.

"Roberta," Bromley softly said. "You are dying, aren't

you?"

"Yes," she replied. There was no point in denying it. She knew that Ashford could smell death on her, could smell how it was rotting her away on the inside.

"I am terribly sorry," Ashford said. "Do they know?"

"It is why they have come here," Roberta explained.

"And now you're turning them into Archers."

"They are Archers," Roberta replied.

She stared at Ashford who had been a friend for many years. He asked no further questions, simply nodded.

"In this doctor's opinion, dear lady, you should not be tree-jumping anymore."

"I know. This was it. My final day in the trees."

"Will I see you again?" Ashford asked.

Roberta shrugged. She looked at him, she looked at the trees around her. She would never be up there anymore. Never. The thought alone was enough to kill her. Ashford seemed to know what she was thinking about. He embraced her, then waved at the children and vanished in the thick of the forest.

Trusting in Ashford's senses, she told the children that they would walk back home instead of taking to the trees. They were nervous at first as they followed Roberta along an animal trail in single file. Eventually, they began to talk and she told them about Ashford Bromley, the doctor of Wychwood. He had come to the forest as a young man and for a while both Archers and elves had feared for his life. But eventually they had discovered that Ashford Bromley didn't need saving. He wasn't strong and he didn't fight.

But he was fast and his senses were in harmony with everything in the forest. He sensed creatures and animals ... and it was those senses that also allowed him to find and use the healing plants. As far as Roberta knew, Ashford hadn't slept in the same place twice and was always ten steps ahead of the redcaps.

"They'd love to get their hands on his skull," she said with a chuckle.

When the children couldn't see it, Roberta angrily punched herself in the chest. The pain was there, stronger now. She felt herself wobble but continued on the trail, hoping that the children behind her wouldn't notice. Roberta wondered just how much longer she'd be able to even walk in the company of her grandchildren. She saw the relief in their eyes when she pushed through an elderberry bush. There was the fence and, beyond it, the safety of the home.

"Quite enough adventure for one day, wouldn't you agree? Let's clean up." She touched the back of her head and sniffed her fingers. "Some of us most definitely need a shower."

CHAPTER TWENTY-ONE

THE BLOOD
AND THE PIKE

When they returned, Corisander didn't need to see the bandage around Roberta's head to know that they had lived through an eventful day. He sensed into them, felt the flow coursing through them sluggishly.

They rappelled down from the oak to land behind the shed. Roberta checked around the corner for Andrew. He was nowhere in sight but Corisander sat there, looking up her stoically.

"Meow," Corisander said.

"Everything's fine," Roberta said, then ushered the children into the shed. Ten minutes later they walked into the house from the front door.

"Dad?" Ellie called.

"Coming!" Andrew called from upstairs.

They heard his footsteps coming down when Milo saw that Roberta still had the bandage around her head. He hurriedly pointed it out. Roberta whipped it away and hid it behind her back as Andrew entered.

"I can't believe you've been out exploring Finstock all day," he said amiably. "Guess the village is a lot more exciting than I thought. You look tired."

"We were everywhere," Nick said.

"Jumped around places," Milo added, with Nick shooting him a glance.

"We walked around the whole of the Oakham Park estate," Roberta said. "Met some interesting people along the way."

"Well, I bet you're hungry. Lily and I made a stew," Andrew said and pointed at a pot on the stove. "You should have seen her. She kept bringing things from your garden, Roberta, and I've just added it all and guess what – it's good!"

Something was happening with Lily, there was no doubt. Corisander felt it more with every day. Slowly, steadily, she was coming back into life and her husband almost shone with joy and relief. Ellie hugged her father impulsively. He embraced her, pulled a leaf from her hair and threw it into the sink.

"Things are good, kids, things are good," he said, then sniffed the air and grimaced. "Before we eat, check your shoes. One of you must have stepped into something."

"Yes, let's put our shoes outside," Roberta said. "And I'll go freshen up," she added with a wink at the children.

Corisander was glad when Roberta had gone upstairs. He had met Ashford Bromley and knew that smell to be from one of the old man's many potions.

Little later Andrew served the children generous helpings of a brownish green stew and they ate ravenously. Roberta joined them with just as much appetite and together they finished the stew, with Roberta wiping the last spot in the pot clean with a thick slice of bread.

"I needed that," Roberta said.

"How are you feeling?" Andrew asked.

"Alive," Roberta said. "Not great, not good, but alive." She stared at her empty plate, then at Andrew, Nick, Milo and Ellie. "I'd love to stick around for another while."

Corisander, on the window sill as always, felt the flow in the room slow and the colors in the air take on melancholy shades. Everyone felt it, even if they couldn't see it as Corisander did. Whatever anyone said and did and even felt, always had a very direct impact on their environment. Humans really did know this to be true and yet they most often reasoned it away. After all, it was "just a feeling."

"It seems that I've successfully managed to mangle the good mood following an exceedingly wonderful meal. Apologies," Roberta said into the silence that had followed her last sentence. "You like stories, don't you?"

"We love them," Andrew said.

"Dad's been telling us all the Irish tales," Ellie said, smiling.

"Still do," Andrew said proudly.

"Wonderful," Roberta said and Corisander wondered what she had in mind. "Just like you, I've always had a love for such stories. And so I have collected them from all over the world. Allow me to show you."

Roberta led them up the stairs into the music room. She walked to the study end of the room where comfortable armchairs were set before a book shelf the size of the wall. It contained everything from travel books to world literature. Andrew and the children had followed Roberta in a state of eagerness, looking forward to a surprise. When they stood before the shelf, their excitement vanished.

"Quite often, in fact, most often, things are not as they seem at first glance," Roberta said, stepped to the shelf and pushed an ornament in the shape of a leaf. The leaf retreated into the wood with a click that activated a mechanism. With a smile and a wink, Roberta stepped back as behind her the shelf opened in the middle like portal doors, revealing another shelf behind it. "It's a bit over the top, I know, but one of our ancestor was a carpenter. He loved building these things. There's one just like it in Oakham Park House."

They all stepped closer and began inspecting the rows and rows of books on the shelf behind the shelf. The books looked old and worn and came in all sizes and faded colors, from rows of large leather-bound volumes to stacks of faded paperbacks. Nick stepped to the far left and peered at the titles.

"These are about Atlantis and here's a section about the Loch Ness monster," he said.

"It's not a monster, it's a dinosaur," Milo replied, still standing at a distance from the shelf. Corisander lay across the doorframe and watched how the boy just stood there, taking in the colors of the countless books, breathing it all in before touching it.

"Actually," Roberta said. "It's a dragon, not a dinosaur."

Milo looked at her in surprise and she gave him a secret wink. Ellie was already sitting on the ground before the shelf, completely engrossed.

"Here's a whole row about fairies," she said, pulled out a book and started looking at page after page, illustration after illustration.

"Will you look at this," Andrew said in amusement. "Here's a section on vampires, nicely sorted by countries. Here's witches and wizards and over here shapeshifters. Roberta, why on Earth are you collecting all of these?"

"Oh, it's always been a fascination of mine," Roberta said as she allowed herself to fall back into one of the armchairs with a contented sigh. She pointed at the second armchair, and Andrew joined her. "Just imagine, Andrew, imagine if all of these were real. It would change the way you'd look at the world, wouldn't it?"

"You believe Atlantis was real?" Andrew said, incredulous.

"Make up your own mind, Andrew," Roberta said. "All the research is there. Or if you're more interested in King Arthur and the Knights of the Round Table, that's over there." Roberta looked at Milo. "Milo? Take a look at the top shelf on the far right. You'll find some excellent books on dwarves."

Milo immediately stepped forward, pulling out book after book.

"Dwarves?" Andrew asked.

"I have research on elves, too, of course," Roberta said.

Andrew just looked at her, at a loss as to what to say. Corisander knew that the man was wondering whether the old woman was crazy.

"You believe in dwarves and elves, too?" Andrew asked.

"Your life, your mind, Andrew. Like I said, make up your own," Roberta replied with a smile. Andrew frowned, shook his head as he looked from Roberta to his three children, all of them with their heads deep in books now. Before he was able to think of a suitable reply, Ellie spoke up without looking away from her book.

"Dad. Just because you haven't seen something, doesn't mean it doesn't exist."

"Well said, Eliza," Roberta said.

As no one seemed interested in further conversation, Andrew eventually picked up a heavy leather covered volume about King Arthur. It was printed in an old font, was filled with handwritten notes and exuded a heavy scent of old paper and mystery. Within moments, Andrew was as captivated as the others.

Corisander walked past Ellie, who was sitting cross-legged in front of the shelf, a fairy book on her knees. She was staring at an illustration of a creature that seemed half fairy, half Chinese dragon with its whiskers, long tail and fiery wings. Corisander had seen many such fairies and had found one last one during his travels across the Xinjiang Province. The fairy had refused to change form. The noise of hordes of humans had driven her into madness. Corisander was there when the fairy killed herself. There was nothing to be done. Nothing to save a glorious creature that now was lost forever. The only thing that remained was this one original drawing in Ellie's hands.

Roberta rose and listened to the perfect silence in the

room. There was nothing but the occasional turning of a page. The darkness beyond the windows was complete. Roberta, tired but content, left the room. In the kitchen, she prepared Roberta Kibble's Famous Book Reading Tea and wondered what would happen with these young Archers when she was gone. She stared into the night at the forest that was out there like a black wall. Three hundred years, generations of Archers. Memories flooded her mind. Laughter in the trees, tears of pain and tears of gratitude, weapons clashing and blood flowing. Let it go, Roberta, she thought to herself. She brought up a tray filled with tea and cups and biscuits and they all helped themselves, mumbling their thanks and returning instantly to their reading.

Milo sat against the wall, several books stacked on the floor next to him. He had fallen into the world of dwarves, their legends, their history, their myths. He had leafed through books narrowly printed in German and showing drawing upon drawing of different kinds of dwarves. Some seemed tiny and some surprisingly tall, some appeared elegant and others looked like beggars. Milo read about the origin of dwarves. According to Norse mythology, they had been created from the flesh of the giant Ymir. He read dwarf stories from Germany to Japan and from Russia to Greece and learned about dwarf kings and peasants, monks and drinkers, miners and animal caretakers. Milo knew that everything he was reading was far more than fairytales. He had seen dwarves. They were real.

Milo discovered one collection of stories about redcaps

entitled "Redcaps – Legends of Bloody Terror". He read page after page and saw that it was just as his grandmother had told them, what was known about redcaps was mostly fanciful. When he came across an illustration, Milo froze. The creature in the picture sat on top of a dead man, lying there in a pool of blood. The dwarf's deep red cap was dripping with the blood of the victim. The redcap, pike in hand, seemed to stare straight at Milo with eyes that shone as red as the bloody cap. The illustration looked nothing like the headhunters of Wychwood ... and yet in those eyes Milo saw Caark and heard his mocking voice, whispering in his ear: "You can't outrun me, boy."

Corisander watched as Roberta stood and walked to Milo. The boy was shivering. She gently took the book from his hands and placed it back on the shelf. She patted his shoulder before arching her back, hear bones cracking precariously.

"It's been a very, very long day," she said. "We should all get some sleep."

Milo nodded and got to his feet. Nick and Ellie put their books back.

"I love these books," Ellie offered and followed it up with a yawn.

Andrew, a book about Arthur Pendragon on his lap, had fallen asleep in his chair. Nick was about to tap him on the shoulder but instead turned to Roberta.

"Grandma, why are all of these books hidden?"

"They're not hidden, my dear," she said tiredly. "I've just not had much use for them these past years, so I put them back there. Let's leave it open. It'll expand your mind … and that of your father," she added with a smile at the sleeping man.

Corisander watched Nick gently tapping his father's shoulder. Andrew woke with a confused snort that made them all smile. He rubbed his eyes, stared at the book and told Roberta how fascinated he was by what he'd read. He left the room still mostly asleep. Corisander felt the heartbeat of the old woman as she shuffled to the door.

The heart was weakening, slowing, and he wondered how much longer she would go on living.

A day, a week, a month perhaps … no more.

CHAPTER TWENTY-TWO

ENCOUNTER
AT THE SOURCE

"I'm not coming," Roberta said.

They had agreed to meet at dawn the next morning. Roberta had prepared sandwiches and tea and together they had walked across the damp grass to the shed. Down in the armory the children had put on their suits while still rubbing sleep from their eyes. It was then that they realized their grandmother wasn't getting ready.

"We're not going in there on our own," Nick said, frowning

"You're ready," Roberta said.

"It's too dangerous," Nick replied.

"I'm a dying old woman, Nick. If anything, I am putting you in danger," Roberta said and turned to the weapons racks. "I've watched you, children. You may lack experience but your instincts are stronger than mine have ever been."

"I don't want to go in there without you," Ellie said.

"Not even to meet the elves?" Roberta asked.

"I do," Milo said instantly. "I want to meet them."

Roberta smiled, then looked from Milo's suit to the weapons rack. She selected two knives and placed them into the empty sheaths sewn into Milo's suit legs. Without a word she showed him how to lock the knives in place. Then she took a small crossbow, added an arrow and shot it without hesitation at the back of the armory. The arrow hit the center of a weathered old target board.

"Nice," Milo said, impressed.

She snapped the crossbow into a strap behind Milo's right shoulder and hooked a patch containing several arrows under his arm.

"You're good to go, Milo," Roberta said. "Who's next?"

Both Ellie and Nick were more reluctant than Milo but the idea of meeting the fabled elves made them step forward, too. Roberta supplied Nick with five knives, sheathed into his suit across the chest. In addition, she took a small hatchet that fit perfectly into the sheath at his right upper arm.

"Give it a try," Roberta suggested.

In one fluid motion Nick whirled around while his left arm pulled the hatchet and threw it against the same target Roberta had used before. The hatchet split the arrow shot by Roberta in two. Even Roberta was impressed.

"I still don't get why I can do that," Nick said.

"You will," Roberta replied.

While Nick went to retrieve his hatchet, Roberta put a small knife on Ellie's hip. She then looked around and settled on two small curved swords. She twirled them in her hands, caught them again with a smile and slipped them into the crossed sheaths on Ellie's back.

"You have tea, you have sandwiches and, in case you

come across any trouble, you have what you need to defend yourself," Roberta said matter-of-factly.

When they stood outside the shed, daylight was already strong and the wet grass was drying fast. Roberta pulled her hand across the grass and showed them her wet palm, explaining that they'd have to be extra careful in the trees for the first hour.

"Got it," Milo said. "So where are the elves?"

"You only find them if they want to be found," Roberta replied.

"I thought we were going to meet them," Ellie said.

"Find Ashford Bromley and give him my regards – and these." She handed Nick a small pouch. "They're his favorite biscuits. Ashford can take you to the elves."

"And how do we find Bromley?" Milo asked.

"Why, you use your senses, of course," Roberta explained. "While that won't work with elves, it most certainly should with Ashford."

"You're not even giving us a direction, right?" Nick asked.

"You're such a smart boy, Nick," Roberta replied.

Nick shook his head, shot his rope and disappeared high up in the oak.

"Have a nice day," Roberta said to Milo and Ellie before they ascended as well.

Roberta couldn't see them anymore but stayed in place for as long as she could still hear them brushing against leaves, jumping on creaking branches … then silence returned. Whether they would meet the elves or not,

Roberta had no way of knowing. All she knew was that she herself hadn't seen them since the death of her brother.

She envied the children.

***

They stood high atop three towering ash trees. Ellie was highest, close to the top of the tree. Her eyes were closed and she clearly enjoyed the sensation of gently swaying back and forth.

"What are we doing again?" Nick asked.

"As far as Dad knows we've gone to a petting zoo in Ramsden," Milo replied.

"There's no way Dad's going to believe that," Nick said.

"Grandma can be pretty convincing," Ellie said, her eyes still closed.

"Petting zoo," Nick said to himself, rolling his eyes. "So, which way do we go? Milo, can you do that thing you do and find the old man?

Milo took a deep breath and closed his eyes. He sensed all sort of wildlife in every direction of Wychwood … but no human beings.

"There's no people anywhere near," Milo said.

"We'll find him," Ellie said confidently, flung her rope and jumped off.

"I guess we'll follow her," Nick said, shrugging.

"I guess so," Milo replied.

They grinned at each other and jumped off after their sister. Just the day before they had witnessed the monstrous redcaps in bloody action and they had seen their grandmother almost break her neck. None of that seemed to have left a mark on them. Armed to their teeth they jumped and swung from tree to tree as if Wychwood had always been their natural habitat.

Hours later they sat in the crown of a beech tree south of Newhill Plain. Wychwood, as small as it really was, seemed to stretch endlessly in every direction. Milo drank some of the tea, then passed the flask on to Nick. Ellie handed out the sandwiches as she looked up at the sun that stood high in the sky.

"Must be around noon," she said.

"Yeah," Milo replied. He was frustrated. He had sensed animals all morning long but every time he thought he sensed something else, it was gone. They had discovered ponds and clearings, creeks and hills … but no Ashford Bromley. Several times he had thought he sensed the old man but that sense always vanished as quickly as it came.

"I read something about springs yesterday," Ellie said.

"Fairy stuff?" Milo asked with little interest.

"Sort of," Ellie replied. "Springs are supposed to be important places. Fairies like them because such places are pure and safe from evil – and they're supposed to have healing powers, too."

"So?" Nick asked.

"So if I were the doctor of the forest, that's where I'd be." She looked from Nick to Milo who suddenly seemed ready to move.

"So where do we find these springs?" he asked.

Nick just lightly shook his head. He rose and smacked the back of Milo's head. Annoyed, Milo followed the others and felt foolish when he realized that they were just returning to the last creek they had crossed. All they had to do was to follow the water to its source. The thinner the creek grew, the most excited the children became.

Ellie, ahead of her brothers by a rope length, suddenly turned in mid-air and alerted the others to stop. Ellie rushed to the thick center of the tree, the others right behind her.

"What is it?" Nick whispered.

"Redcaps?" Milo added. He focused his senses and, as he did, his eyes narrowed. What he sensed was nothing had had sensed before.

Ellie was agitated, gesturing for them to shut up and wait.

Then they all saw it. A large black creature approached the creek. It peered in every direction, then stooped to drink. The creature moved with a feline quality but was larger even than a panther. With its thick black fur and massive bear-like head it looked like pure menace. Then, as suddenly as it had appeared, it vanished again. As if it had heard something, it lifted its head and bounded off into the bushes.

"That was the Black Beast," Nick whispered, stunned.

"You'd think Grandma would have mentioned something like that," Milo suggested.

"That was the Black Beast!" Nick exclaimed again.

"What now?" Ellie asked.

"Nothing's changed," Milo replied. "Can't be far to the

source."

When they swung into an alder tree moments later, they saw a small clearing below. If they had expected something special, they were disappointed. Water bubbled up from a fist-sized hole in the clearing with an occasional gurgling sound. The water leaked from the spring across muddy ground to form the miniscule beginning of the creek.

There, stretched out on his back right beside the spring, lay Ashford Bromley, asleep with a content smile on his face.

"We have to warn him about the Black Beast," Nick whispered back urgently.

"It's coming," Milo said, pointing down the creek where the big black creature was on a direct path to Bromley, one stalking step at a time. Milo pulled the crossbow from his back, his fingers nervously readying an arrow.

"It's the Black Beast, Milo," Nick said, incredulous. "That's like killing Bigfoot!"

"Mr. Bromley! Wake up. Please wake up!" Ellie called down.

"Black Beast!" Nick shouted.

There was no reaction from the sleeping man by the spring. Unnerved, Nick jumped from branch to branch and landed in between Bromley and the Black Beast. He pulled a knife and the hatchet and crouched into a fighting stance. Milo and Ellie jumped to stand on either side of Nick, forming a protective shield in front of Bromley.

"If any of you hurt Jim Jam, I'll be very upset," Bromley said behind him. When they looked at him, he was sitting upright, the wooden staff laid across his lap.

"Jim Jam?" Ellie asked, scared stiff as the big creature slunk around them, never letting them out of its sight, then lying down next to Bromley.

"Please, put your weapons away. You're making him very uncomfortable."

Slowly, uneasily, Nick, Milo and Ellie sheathed their arms. Ellie remembered the pouch she had carried with her and held it up.

"Grandma asked us to bring you these," Ellie said, handing him the biscuits. He opened the pouch, ate a biscuit and then tossed one to Jim Jam. Lightning-fast, the creature exposed its fangs, snatched the biscuit in mid-air, then lay down again.

"Thank you … Ellie. It is Ellie, isn't it?"

"The Black Beast … nuts," Nick said, completely in awe.

"He really doesn't appreciate being called that, you know," Bromley said. "Now please, join me." Bromley pointed to the place on the other side of the spring. Awkwardly, the children sat, unable to take their eyes off the big black creature. "And do stop staring at him. That's just impolite."

"Shouldn't we be up in the trees?" Milo asked.

"I do understand your concern about certain headhunters, but springs are fairly safe," Bromley explained. "It's not so much that redcaps couldn't kill us here, it's just that they can't stand the purity of such places. This is Wort's Well, by the way."

"And I bet they're not too crazy about meeting Jim Jam

151

either," Nick said.

"Indeed," Bromley said with a grin. "Jim Jam certainly isn't your average fairy."

"That's a fairy?" Ellie asked, stunned.

Jim Jam flopped to the side, eyes closed. The cow-like tongue explored his nostrils. The creature didn't look quite as ferocious as it had moments earlier.

"Of course he is. What did you think he was? The whole notion of fairies being ethereal little butterfly creatures is just silly. Think about it! You do know about the flow, don't you?"

"Grandma told us about it," Milo said.

"Good, good, where was I? Ah yes, Jim Jam. As you know, when the noise became too much, there were those who adapted to survive. Some fairies became rocks, others trees – and many chose animal form. In the case of Jim Jam, alas, he couldn't make up his mind until it was too late to switch. He ended up being stuck in the forms he had been playing around with. If you've ever heard of Pegasus, the Chimaera or the Griffin – same thing."

As Bromley talked, Jim Jam stood up, yawned and stretched, then walked to Ellie where he lay down again, his thick fur against her leg. With a nod, Bromley encouraged her to pet the creature and when she did, Jim Jam closed his eyes and purred.

"He's wonderful," Ellie softly said as not to disturb Jim Jam.

"Well then, what can I do for you?"

"Grandma said you could take us to the elves," Ellie said.

"I could do that, certainly," Bromley said while scratching his scruffy beard. "But what makes you think they want to see you?"

"We're Archers," Milo replied.

"Yes, there is that. But you are also strangers," Bromley said. "The elves don't like strangers. Especially not strangers of the human race. You must remember that everything they've lived through these past three thousand years was brought on by the noisers. That's us, by the way. Humans – we're the noisers."

"I still want to meet them," Milo said.

"Me, too," Ellie said, still stroking Jim Jam's fur. The creature lifted its head and seemed to nod at Bromley.

"Well, if that's what you want," Bromley said and nimbly jumped to his feet. The moment he did, Jim Jam was up as well and the children scrambled to follow suit.

Bromley stuck another biscuit into his mouth, then adjusted the shoulder pouch, motioned for them to follow him and stalked off into the wood.

PROTECTORS
OF WYCHWOOD

They moved in single file through the thick undergrowth beyond Wort's Well. Jim Jam was out of sight, silently shadowing them. Bromley had informed them that the animals in the forest were behaving strangely and that they should be alert. Then he asked them walk in silence – after a few minutes, he suddenly stopped and turned.

"Look, I know you're Archers and you're pretty good for beginners but would you mind not making so much noise? You're as loud as a stomping colony of rabbits in spring. Just, you know, have your ropes ready. With all the racket we may get company. If you feel you should be in the tree, don't wait, don't ask, just trust your instinct and go."

They continued deeper and deeper into a part of the forest that seemed entirely unfamiliar to the children. Nick jumped and swung into a tree when a pheasant nearby called out, probably startled by Jim Jam.

Bromley just looked up, shook his head and continued. Nick jumped back down and found himself staring at Milo's grinning face.

"What?" Nick growled.

"You're a little … jumpy," Milo said, grinning even more

broadly. And Ellie, standing right behind Milo, had to stifle a laugh.

"Har, har," Nick said, pushing past them to follow Bromley.

"Mr. Bromley said that was a pheasant," Ellie said, walking closely behind Nick with Milo bringing up the rear.

"They're sort of like chicken," Milo added.

"Oh, shut up," Nick hissed.

Up ahead Bromley stopped at a towering tree. Its trunk was tightly overgrown with ivy that snaked up beyond the foliage of the tree.

"This is Hawksnest," Bromley said, his hand on the tree. "It's one of twelve observation posts the elves use. You see the ivy? For some reason, ivy's always been attracted to fairy creatures. If you see places covered in ivy you can be sure there's something there.

"Are they up there now?" Milo whispered.

"If they were, they wouldn't want to be disturbed during their watch," Bromley said. He waved them on. Milo glanced back once more. Now that Bromley had revealed the observation post and explained the ivy, the tree stood out clearly from all those around it. He wanted to climb up, jump up, swing up so badly. He wanted to see who was up there and wondered whether the Archers had protected the forest from up there, too. He turned just in time to see the others disappear down a slope and hurried after them.

They crossed to the left of a little pond, small enough to vault across. Half of it was covered by reed, the other half seemed more mud than water. Bromley advised against walking to close to the edge. While the pond was shallow, one never knew what might live in there. The children took another step back.

"The only fairy beings I've ever met in the forest were elves, redcaps and Jim Jam," Bromley said and a low growl answered him from somewhere on the left. "But I've always felt that there are more creatures within the dome. Whatever they are, wherever they are, they are as much in prison as the others."

Bromley stopped and turned to look at them.

"On days like these there's an easy way to know whether fairy creatures are near."

"How?" Ellie eagerly asked.

"When there's no wind, look around yourself. If you see a single leaf fluttering, then you know. You're in the presence of a fairy."

Both boys found a fluttering leaf highly suspect as proof, but Ellie was already looking across the dense undergrowth for movement. When she spotted a single leaf on a hazel bush fluttering wildly, she grabbed Milo's arm and pointed.

"There!" she whispered.

"I don't see anything," Milo said with little interest.

"No, we don't," Bromley said. "But they see us."

Bromley continued leading them through dense forest and at times it felt as if they were zig-zagging and circling, walking past familiar places. Bromley told them that the cave of the redcaps was nearby. Apparently, the redcaps had, over the course of the past three thousand years, built extensive caves and underground tunnels. Bromley told the children that the general location of their main halls was known but that the dwarves had countless ways out of their tunnels. They could appear out of the ground anywhere and anytime.

They seemed to be in the darkest part of Wychwood when Bromley finally stopped. Here, in this part of the wood, the children discovered a glimpse of what remained of the glorious ancient forest. Everything here seemed bigger. Trees stood tall and blocked out the sun. Immense roots lay everywhere like the gnarled fingers of giants. Dark green moss seemed to embrace fallen trees and large ferns stood like silent sentinels. Bromley and the children stood in front of a group of enormous beeches.

"We're here," Bromley said, pointing up. "You wanted to see the elves, didn't you? Well then, up you go."

They climbed as quickly as they could, anxious to see the elves. Would they live as the children had read about in books and seen in films? Would they find a beautifully carved tree house up there? When they cautiously pushed their heads through the canopy, they saw five hammocks, made of dark cloth and vines, hanging at different levels like clusters of bird nests. All but one appeared empty. The lowest of the hammocks sagged greatly under the weight of a large and rotund elf. Eyes closed, he was chewing ecstatically into a chocolate bar, half devouring the wrapper without noticing.

"... Um, hello?" Nick asked.

The elf opened his eyes, saw the children and gagged on the chocolate bar. Trying to sit up in the hammock, the elf coughed again and again until he wobbled out of the hammock and fell backwards, through the branches and out of sight.

"I see you've met Anthor," a gentle voice said.

They all spun around to see the head of another elf peer down at them from one of the hammocks. The gray-haired elf sat up and quizzically looked down at them as the one named Anthor swung back into view. He moved with surprising elegance and flung himself into a sitting position on a nearby branch.

"Who are you and what are you doing here?" Anthor asked with an eager look on his face. "But, more importantly, do you have any food on you? Sweets, chocolate, biscuits?"

The children were still speechless when Bromley climbed into view, breathing heavily.

"Ashford," said the old elf, "good to see you."

"Likewise, O'Rein, likewise," Bromley said, still catching his breath. "Pardon the intrusion but you'll understand in a moment. All right, introductions – you are going to love this."

"You must be Lily's children," O'Rein said before Bromley had a chance to explain.

"Yes," Milo said, "We're Archers."

"We're actually Murphys," Ellie said.

"But yes, we're Lily's children," Nick explained. "I'm Nick, this is Ellie and I guess you already know about Milo."

"I haven't had the pleasure," O'Rein said. He lithely

jumped from his hammock and sat close to them. "Why do you think I might know this young man?"

"I met Shendak," Milo explained. "I met Caark, too – I punched him," Milo added.

O'Rein looked from one to the other in silence. His eyes were an emerald green that sparkled with wisdom and kindness.

"Well, let me at least introduce you," Bromley began again and pointed at Anthor. "This is Anthor. Watch your food when he's near. And this gentleman is O'Rein. They call him "O'Rein the Wise" but the reason for it eludes me," Bromley added.

O'Rein just smiled.

"Nick, Milo, Ellie," Anthor said. "It is very nice to meet the children of Lily Archer. Now, do you have any food on you?"

Bromley sighed, pulled Roberta's biscuits from his pouch and tossed them to Anthor. The big elf, looking at the children with hungry hope in his eyes, caught the biscuits with complete ease. He leaned back and ate them slowly, bit by small bit, his eyes closed, savoring every bite.

"Roberta makes the best biscuits in the world," Anthor murmured.

"I did not know that Lily had children," O'Rein said.

"We live in America," Nick explained.

"But you're here now," O'Rein stated. "And you're tree-jumping."

"Grandma asked us to come," Ellie offered. "And she told us about the Archers and the tree-jumping and we could just do it."

"I am not entirely surprised. How is Roberta?" O'Rein asked.

"Don't you know?" Nick asked back.

"I'm afraid we've not been in contact since the death of her brother Chester," O'Rein explained.

"Wasn't that thirty years ago?" Milo wanted to know.

"Yes," O'Rein replied. "What is wrong with Roberta?"

"She's dying," Bromley blurted. "Cancer. It's a human thing."

"I am very sorry," O'Rein said, tears forming in his eyes. "Roberta has been a dear friend for many, many years."

"What's going on here?" a sonorous voice commanded. He had appeared seemingly out of nowhere. Standing high up in the nearest tree stood Shendak. He jumped across and everyone except for O'Rein stiffened. There was something undeniably severe about Shendak.

"They're Archers, Shendak," Anthor said eagerly.

"I know that," Shendak replied indifferently. "Why are they here?"

"We are protectors of the forest," Milo said. "Just like you."

"Well, they are Archers," Anthor said again.

"Fiveoak. Go," Shendak said to Anthor. The big elf gave a start, as if struck by lightning. He nodded, sent the children a parting smile, then flung his rope and jumped. An instant later he had swung out of sight.

Shendak stepped to Milo and leaned in close, staring at him.

"You think you have a right to be here?" Shendak said.

"Yes," Milo said.

"Did your grandmother tell you how many of us died because of her?"

The children looked at each other in confusion.

"This is not their story," O'Rein interjected gently.

"They are Archers, are they not?" Shendak shot at him. He turned back to the children. "Do as you will but do not get in our way. The friendship that once was between us is no more. Now leave."

"I would advise –" O'Rein began but was interrupted instantly.

"I want them gone," Shendak ordered.

"They call me the Wise One, Shendak. And I do believe that my thoughts have been of value once or twice in the past."

"Say what you have to say," Shendak said.

"These children, Shendak, they are Archers and they are more than that," O'Rein said. "Can't you feel it? There is something about them that is … different."

Shendak shook his head in irritation as if unwilling to contemplate anything beyond his decision. Then he abruptly looked at the children again.

"Did Roberta send you here?"

"She … she thought we might like to meet you," Nick said.

"I wanted to meet you," Ellie added.

"It was her idea. All of this," Shendak said. "It's still all about the head. She's trying to use the children. That's what all of this is about and I know you see that, too, oh Wise One," he added with a smirk at O'Rein.

"What are you talking about?" Nick asked.

"Ask your grandmother," Shendak said and turned away from them.

"I think we should go," Ellie said.

Milo glared at Shendak as they rose. He was about to speak when Shendak spun around.

"Maple Hill!" he yelled, ran and jumped at the same time. A split second later, O'Rein followed him. They watched the two elves swing out of sight.

"Well, that's that," Bromley said. "You wanted to meet the elves, you've met the elves. Now I suggest you leave before Shendak returns."

"What was that all about?" Nick asked.

"Ask your grandmother," Bromley said just as Shendak had.

Without a word, Milo ran and jumped where moments before Shendak and O'Rein had leaped away from.

"What are you doing?" Ellie called.

"Maple Hill!" Milo called back.

"Bad idea! Don't go there!" Bromley yelled after him.

Ellie and Nick readied their ropes to jump after Milo.

"Why? What's happening there?" Nick hurriedly asked Bromley.

"Same thing that happens every time. People wander into the forest. Redcaps try to kill them. Elves try to stop that from happening," Bromley explained.

Before he had finished his sentence, Ellie and Nick had

jumped off to follow Milo. Bromley sighed, then shrugged and made himself comfortable in Anthor's hammock.

***

Trying to catch up with the elves seemed impossible but Milo's senses guided him toward a place where he felt a man in shock. Nick and Ellie right behind him, he stopped in the upper branches of a linden tree.

Hidden behind dense foliage, they peered down and saw Shendak, O'Rein and a third, bald-headed elf, beating back three redcaps. The redcaps all looked as filthy, as squat and as powerful as Caark had looked. The dwarves were trying to reach a man who lay, sprawled and dazed, on the forest floor.

"It's Christopher Smith," Nick whispered.

"We have to do something," Milo said.

"We stay," Ellie said firmly. "Look, the elves are winning."

The fight below was an even one with the raw power of the dwarves matched by the skills of the elves. Metal was smashed against metal, swords, knives and axes were swung and all the while the redcaps aimed to kill whereas the elves just tried to keep them in check. Little by little the elves managed to push the furious redcaps further away from Smith.

"There's another one," Nick said, horrified.

Just a few steps behind Smith a hatch in the ground was opened and a fourth redcap climb out. Milo noticed that, at the end of his right arm, the dwarf had a hook instead of a hand. Without thinking, Milo jumped.

The fourth redcap stared in disbelief when he suddenly saw a boy standing in between him and his prey. He grunted and ran at Milo, fast as a boar and all Milo could do was to duck away from the hook that grazed his cheek. The redcap rammed Milo, swiped him out of the way and reached for Christopher Smith.

"Milo, watch out!" Nick called. Milo rolled out of the way as Nick threw one of his knives and buried it in the redcap's shoulder. Furious, the dwarf reached back, tore the knife out and threw it away.

"Come down and try that again. Come on. Let me take your head!" he shouted up at Nick. The redcap looked from Nick to Milo to his intended victim. Then, from the corner of his eye he saw the bald elf running his way.

The redcap weighed his chances, jumped back into the hole and slammed the hatch shut.

CHAPTER TWENTY-FOUR

OF GIFTS
AND ANOMALIES

"They are real," Smith stammered. "They … they are real! I … I know you," he said to Milo and was stunned when Nick and Ellie sailed down next him. "You're the Archer children. I told you about the monsters. You see? I'm not crazy. It's all – all of this – it's all real," he said as he scrambled to his feet.

Milo smiled at Ellie with unmistakable pride while Nick went to pick up the knife the redcap had thrown away. He recovered it, wiped the dwarf blood off and returned it to its proper place.

"You saved my life," Smith said to the children.

"Everything is okay now," Ellie replied soothingly.

Smith's eyes opened wide when he saw the three elves coming toward them.

Shendak ignored the children.

O'Rein gave them a quick smile while the third elf showed no emotion at all. The third elf was as tall as Shendak, but broader, and his bald head and face were crisscrossed with scars.

"We saved him" Milo said, trying to sound like a calm protector of Wychwood.

Shendak didn't say a word. He blew powder into the face of Christopher Smith. As Smith's eyes glazed over, Shendak caught him in his arms. Then the elf ran off as if the human being in his arms were weightless. He jumped up into the trees and was gone.

"We are protectors of the forest as much as he is and if he doesn't like it that's his problem!" Milo shouted after Shendak.

"What's going to happen to Smith?" Nick asked.

"The same thing that happens about once a week, Nick," O'Rein explained. "Smith comes looking for monsters. Sometimes they find him. Then we save him, wipe his memory and drop him where he came in. Well, this is Culanxan the Brave," O'Rein said. "And these are Ellie, Milo and Nick Archer ... Murphy," he added with a wink in Ellie's direction.

"We should go," Culanxan evenly said.

"I'd like to show you something first," O'Rein said, pointing at Milo. "Milo here managed to get away from Caark by punching him in the face."

"Show me," Culanxan said.

Milo looked from the powerfully built elf to O'Rein in confusion.

"Punch him," O'Rein said to Milo. "As hard as you can."

"I don't know what happened there," Milo said. "It's different, I don't know how to do what I did there."

"Just punch him," O'Rein said.

Frustrated, Milo threw a punch at Culanxan's stomach. The elf didn't move and didn't blink – and Milo shook his hand in pain.

"Again," O'Rein suggested.

Milo threw another punch but this time Culanxan had moved before his fist hit the target. Milo punched again and missed. With every punch Culanxan easily moved out of the way. Milo felt his temper rise with every empty punch, he felt his himself boiling and then he threw another punch. It hit Culanxan squarely in the gut and the big elf was lifted off his feet and landed flat on the ground. Stunned, Culanxan lay there for a moment, then he calmly came back to his feet and gave O'Rein a simple nod.

"Remarkable," he said. "What about the others?"

"From the little I have seen I'd say that Nick has the Eye and Ellie has the Air," O'Rein said.

"What are you talking about?" Nick asked.

"I'm talking about gifts. Milo, you have the Rage. It is a rare manifestation of the flow. You may have heard of Cuchulainn?"

"Of course, my favorite Irish hero," Milo said.

"He had the Rage, just like you," O'Rein said.

"The Rage ..." Milo said quietly.

"And you, Nick, from what I can tell you have perfect aim, that's what we call The Eye. And Ellie, yours is The Air, you have a sense of balance that is surpassed only by flying. Why you have these gifts is a mystery to me."

Culanxan lightly frowned, looking at them one by one. Then he tilted his head.

"There is an intrusion at Lankridge. He put a hand on Milo's shoulder and gave him a nod as if it were a salute.

"Archers, farewell," he added crisply before swinging off into the trees.

"Do you sense everyone coming into Wychwood?" Ellie asked.

"Not always, I'm afraid," O'Rein replied. "If you wish, I will walk with you for a while. It is safe for now."

"Where to?" Milo asked suspiciously.

"Home," O'Rein said. "You have saved a man's life today. I believe you deserve a warm dinner and a good night's rest … and I'm sure your grandmother will be eager to hear about your day."

The moment O'Rein said it, they felt the tiredness in their bones. The thought of dinner in Grandma's cozy kitchen made them smile. They followed O'Rein along a deer trail. Without realizing it, their senses remained on the alert and their hands close to their weapons.

"May I ask you something?" Ellie asked O'Rein as the path widened and they were able to walk next to each other.

"Of course."

"Are there any more elves out in the world?"

"I wouldn't know … I doubt it," O'Rein said and sighed. "I have often listened beyond the dome but have heard nothing but the noise of humanity. For all I know, out there, there's nothing left other than a few anomalies."

"Anomalies?" Ellie asked.

"Like this one," O'Rein said and pointed at Corisander, who sat waiting on the other side of the fence. Deep in conversation, the children only now noticed that they had arrived.

"The cat's an anomaly?" Nick asked. "Why?"

"Corisander is a fairy," O'Rein said and knelt down, only the fence separating him from the cat. "He should long be dead. Instead he lives out there, immortal among you all."

"Meow," Corisander said and O'Rein smiled.

"Nice to see you, too, old friend," O'Rein said.

Shielded by the shed, the children used their ropes to vault the fence and land softly on the other side. Ellie was quick to pet Corisander.

"You're a fairy," she said, grinning happily. Corisander didn't mind the attention.

"Well done, Archers. May our paths cross again," O'Rein said and readied himself to leap off into the trees.

"Can I ask you one more thing?" O'Rein nodded as they approached the fence and Milo continued. "When we jump we just sort of feel everything around us … is that a gift, too?"

"No, those are just our elfish senses, Milo."

Milo looked at him in confusion.

"But we're not …" Milo began.

"My goodness," O'Rein exclaimed. "Roberta hasn't told you? The Archers have elfish blood. How else do you think you are able to do what you're doing?"

"We're part elf?" Nick asked, perplexed.

"Welcome to the family," O'Rein said, winked and vanished into the depths of Wychwood.

CHAPTER TWENTY-FIVE

THE OLD KING

He had been thrilled by the presence of the younglings, by the rejuvenating energy they had brought into the forest. But he had not understood before now.

Once upon a time the Old King had felt into everything. Once upon a time knowledge had been irrelevant. Now he needed to know. He needed to understand the world he had woken into. It seemed wrong – his need to know, to make sense.

It was something that had not been necessary in the time before time.

The Old King was displeased, but there seemed to be no other way in a world that was distorted by human beings. A world that was … wrong.

He now began to understand the power that radiated from the younglings. They had met the elves and the old man by the well and they had fought once more.

The Old King feared for their lives, lives that felt inextricably linked with his and he became angry at the thought that anyone might harm them.

As the trees shook around him, he realized that it was he who was shaking the trees.

And the Old King wondered.

CHAPTER TWENTY-SIX

SEA WARRIORS

The rest of the day was an unusual one for Corisander.

He was used to being the cat, appreciated, occasionally caressed, but mostly left to his own devices. Corisander knew that the children would never see him as a cat anymore.

He wondered whether, now that they knew he was a fairy, Nick would still give him belly rubs. It really was one of the best things about having the form of a cat.

The three children had gone down into the armory. They returned their weapons and climbed out of their suits. Nick wiped the used knife once more, deep in thought as he looked at the cloth that came away with a reddish hue.

"What are you thinking about?" Milo asked.

"Blood," Nick replied.

"We'll have to ask Grandma about that," Ellie exclaimed brightly, misinterpreting Nick's thoughts. "I can't believe we're part elf!"

"Yeah," Nick murmured.

Nick left the armory last. He looked around and Corisander could feel the weight of the history, the ancestry, the responsibilities and the recent revelations laying heavy on the boy. He turned off the light and locked the door. Nick noticed that Corisander sat at his feet.

"So, you're a fairy, huh?"

Corisander rolled onto his back. Nick kneeled down, paused for a moment, then proceeded to deliver a first-rate belly rub. Corisander purred contentedly, glad to know that belly rubs would continue to be delivered.

While they had been in the forest, their grandmother had been busy. The table on the patio was beautifully set for tea, with a cake beckoning from underneath a glass dome.

Roberta was on the side of the house where a new patch had been dug and lined with wooden boards. Both she and Lily were inside the patch, on their knees, planting lavender bushes. When Roberta saw them, she smiled broadly, rose to her feet and waved her dirt-caked hands.

"How was your day?"

"Eventful," Nick said.

"Where's Dad?" Milo asked.

"He told me that he's on a deadline to finish an article for the newspaper. Since there's no connection here, he went to the village library."

Ellie sat in the grass next to where Lily was digging another hole. Her mother's eyes were focused on the earth before her. It was as it always was, she didn't even seem to know that others were around her.

"Why's Mom doing this?"

"Well, because I told her," Roberta replied. "We didn't exactly have a conversation about it, mind you. I just thought it might be something nice for us to do and when I started, she joined me. Now then, did you find Ashford?"

"At Wort's Well," Nick said. "We also found the Black

Beast," he added with a smirk.

"I thought you might like to see him," Roberta said with a grin.

The Black Beast … Corisander lay down by the corner of the house. A good place to keep an eye on both the forest and the Archers. Corisander knew that he would have almost ended up a dual form like Jim Jam. Luckily, he had chosen his final shape just in time. For a while he had been torn between the forms of a cat and that of a stork … compared to a majestic dual form like the Griffin's, his would have been a fairly odd combination.

While Lily planted more lavender bushes, Roberta found herself captivated by the retelling of the children's adventures. They had met the elves, big Anthor, wise O'Rein, severe Shendak and cool Culanxan. They had defied Shendak and, by doing so, had saved the life of Christopher Smith.

"This scratch?" Milo said proudly, touching his cheek. "A present from the cap's hook, just before Nick got him."

"That redcap's name is Urk and the reason he has a hook where once he had a hand, well, he wouldn't let go. What was I supposed to do?" Roberta said evenly.

"You chopped it off?" Milo asked, clearly awestruck.

"They called me Hatchet for a reason," Roberta said with a grin, before pointing at Milo's cheek. "We'll put something on that. By the time your father's back it will be as new."

Nick climbed one of the carved rocks and sat.

"Grandma. How come you didn't mention that we're

173

elfish?" he asked.

"You had to discover your talents and meet the elves. Otherwise how could you possibly have believed something like this? Now, now it all makes sense, doesn't it?"

"True," Nick said. "… Shendak says you sent us because of your brother's head."

"That's …" Roberta began angrily, then sighed. "… only partially true. I wanted you to see an Archer's world and I really wanted you to meet the elves. But it is also true that I cannot bury Chester without his head. I've asked the elves, time and time again, to help me recover it but they are unwilling to go down into the tunnels. Alone I stand no chance."

"He said elves have died because of you," Milo said.

"Elves have died for thousands of years," she replied severely. "Ever since they were imprisoned in the forest, their whole existence has been about fighting the redcaps. Shendak claims that some of them died because I risked too much."

"Did you?"

"… Yes," Roberta said softly. "… I wasn't thinking clearly for a long time after Chester's death. I blamed the elves. I blamed my parents. I even blamed Lily … the truth is that it was my fault. My fault that Chester died. My fault that his head is down there."

Corisander saw that she was close to tears and so did the children. None of them felt like pressing their grandmother for more. Without a word, Ellie approached

174

and embraced Roberta and for a while the old woman's tears flowed in silence.

"When I was little O'Rein told me that the tears we cry are drops of the flow," Roberta finally said, sniffling. Ellie released her from the hug and Roberta gratefully smiled at her. "I always liked that thought."

An hour later they all sat on the patio.

The children had showered and the scratch across Milo's cheek had almost disappeared thanks to Roberta Kibble's Famous Healing Balm. Andrew had returned from the library, complaining about the terrible internet connection, but he had finally managed to send his article just in time. Lily sat in one of the armchairs, gazing out at Wychwood and smiling.

And Corisander? He purred in Nick's lap and wondered. The children had told Roberta about their gifts, the Air, the Eye and the Rage. Corisander had always known about such gifts, abilities that came about only in the rarest of circumstances. To have three such circumstances with three children of the same family … it left Corisander with only one conclusion – it had something to do with their parents.

Corisander watched Andrew feed Lily small bits of cake. She ate and she enjoyed it, as Corisander sensed. And yet there was no awareness of Andrew. Lily remained elsewhere and wherever that was, Corisander could not tell. In his view, she was an Archer and was the reason for the children's elfish blood.

It had been with Robert the Archer's daughter that

Shendak had fallen in love with all those many years ago. Two sons were born and their elfish abilities were carried through all future generations … Corisander took a closer look at Andrew who was a Murphy, an ancestor of ones who had called themselves sea warriors.

The sea.

It occurred to Corisander that Andrew didn't only shower every morning, he also showered every night before going to sleep. And he often stepped away to wash his face, to "cool down", as he called it. Andrew set the plate with the remaining crumbs of cake back onto the table. He took a pitcher, filled a glass with water and drank it in one thirsty gulp. He filled the glass again and emptied it once more. What if, Corisander asked himself, what if it was to do with the sea?

He felt more deeply into the man then and followed the distant echo of the flow … until he knew.

Without meaning to, they had all drifted to the library after dinner. Sitting in chairs and against the walls, the children poured over stories that made sense to them now. With what they knew, they were now easily able to separate truth from fiction.

"Says here that dwarves turn to stone in daylight," Milo said, shaking his head and flicking to the next page of his book.

"And did you know that elves and fairies don't like iron?" Nick said without lifting his eyes from the book on his lap.

"Yes, I read that," Ellie said, giggling with a glance in

Corisander's direction. "I've also found out that fairies are so tiny and fast that we can't see them. Oh, and they make fairy dust in fairy land."

Corisander, curled up in Roberta's lap, didn't even dignify it with a meow. He looked at Andrew who frowned at his children.

"Since when are you all this interested in fantasy stuff?" he asked.

"Well, we're here and the books are here and there's no internet," Milo replied casually. "We have to do something, right?"

"Right," Andrew said. "Well, it makes me happy. I can't remember the last time I saw Nick with a book in his hands – I mean before coming here. Makes me cry to think that one day the printing presses around the globe will stop. It really does. But I'm afraid it's inevitable. The signs are everywhere. Unfortunately, that's the way of the world. The old always has to make way for the new."

In the silence that followed, Andrew sagged in his chair. Roberta reached across to the tea table between their chairs. The tea was there, the cups were ready. Carefully, she poured two cups and handed one of them to Andrew.

"Roberta Kibble's Famous Book Reading Tea?" Andrew asked.

"Roberta Kibble's Famous Spirit Lifter," she replied with a smile.

He couldn't help smiling and the smile spread further when the first drops of Roberta's tea pearled down his throat.

"Talking about books," Roberta said. "You've seen that Tolkien's books are on that shelf. He's been here."

"Seriously?" Andrew asked, stunned. "J.R.R. Tolkien was here?"

"Yes," Roberta said. "And so was C.S. Lewis, just so you know. They came to this place because they had heard of the many tales of Wychwood. The stories they told – where do you think they got their inspirations from?"

Corisander saw the children gaping at their grandmother. Obviously, they had read some of these authors' books.

And Corisander could see their minds racing through their memories and discovering the flow in the stories of Tolkien and Lewis. In fact, Corisander had spent time with both of them and Tolkien especially had somehow felt that there was more to this cat than met the eye.

Corisander jumped from Roberta's lap and surprised them all by jumping up onto the book shelf. He knew what he was looking for.

"I think he wants to read a little, too," Andrew said with a grin. To his surprise, no one found it amusing. They were all intently staring at the cat.

Corisander clawed at a thin book, then pulled it out of the shelf and dropped it to the floor. He jumped down next to it and looked at Andrew.

"I think Corisander wants you to read it," Nick said evenly. He exchanged glances with Ellie and Milo. Roberta lightly shrugged as if to say, I have no idea what he's up to.

Andrew picked up the book and the moment he did, Corisander jumped back onto Roberta's lap, curled up and closed his eyes. Job done, he thought.

"Tales of the Selkie People," Andrew said, reading the book's cover as he sat down again.

"Seal people," Ellie said. "Right?"

"Right," Andrew replied. "My granddad told me about them. Seal-like creatures who can take on human form."

"And when they did," Roberta mused, "they sometimes married humans. What did your ancestors do for a living, Andrew?"

"They were fishermen," Ellie said instead of her father. She eagerly looked from him to her brothers and back. "Tell us one of the stories, Dad."

"Sure, why not," Andrew said, a bit confused by the solemnity in the room. He flipped through the pages, settled on one and began. "This one's called Seven Tears ... Beneath the sea there once was a kingdom of fairy people. They looked like humans, but were far more beautiful. Within their kingdom, there was air to breathe. However, to travel from their kingdom to the land above, they changed into the shape of seals."

Andrew went on to tell a story Corisander knew to be true. As always, some of it had been transformed into elements of fairytale whimsy, but the core was true - stories of fishermen and widows falling in love with beautiful selkie people. And one day, often after raising the children, the selkies would return to their home in the sea, far away from the noise.

As Andrew read the story, Corisander felt the heartbeats of the children quicken.

Roberta smiled at them and a sense of flow surged through the room as they realized that both their parents might have the blood of fairies coursing through their veins.

"Beautiful story," Andrew said as he closed the book. "Sad but beautiful."

Ellie just looked at him and nodded, a smile playing around her lips.

"What?" Andrew asked.

"Meow," Corisander replied and yawned.

They laughed and rose and Roberta tightly hugged Corisander – something he didn't particularly appreciate but he knew that it gave her strength and so he allowed it.

"Time for bed. Big day tomorrow," Roberta said with flourish. "For tomorrow, we shall visit Lord Francis Thornton."

CHAPTER TWENTY-SEVEN

LORD
FRANCIS THORNTON

They were the same age and many people expected them to one day be married. But one was an Archer, the other a Thornton. Their paths rarely crossed as they got older and she would think about him as she jumped from tree to tree and he would think about her as he jumped from university to university. Roberta never regretted marrying Henry Kibble … but she also never forgot about the times before then with the man who would one day become Lord Francis Thornton of Oakham Park.

This was the day she would introduce the family to her old friend. For the particular occasion, she wanted to look and feel her best … in as much as that was still possible, she thought grimly. It was early morning and she was in the forest to find a few special herbs and a particular root that would give her strength through the day.

Roberta was on her knees, digging in the shadow of a young beech. The morning light gave everything around her crisp clarity.

She smiled at the colors of the leaves, brightly illuminated by the rays of the sun. She should have paid attention instead.

"Hatchet," a rough voice said.

Roberta turned and saw that Gerg, a redcap with an eyepatch, stood no more than ten paces from her. Roberta put her basket aside and dropped the trowel she had used for digging next to it. She got to her feet without pause. She knew that the show of weakness meant sudden death. Gerg just stood there, with both hands leaning on his pike, eyeing her.

"Gerg," Roberta greeted calmly.

"I have been waiting for your head."

"We all have to die sometime," Roberta replied. "Today is your day."

She simply stood, breathing calmly. There was no fear, there was no anger. She knew that she would not have the strength to defeat the mighty Gerg, he who had killed her brother, taken his head, laughing.

"You are alone," Gerg said.

"As are you," she replied.

Gerg sniffed the air. Roberta could see that he was contemplating attacking the famed Hatchet. She had killed seven of his comrades. She had maimed many more. She had been a fighter more fierce than the elves. He knew all of that. And it made him cautious.

"You look weak, old woman."

"Come then," Roberta offered evenly. "Come dance with the old woman."

She put a hand onto the hatchet, but did not remove it from her belt. She simply wanted Gerg to follow her hand, to see the hatchet. Roberta smiled and closely watched

Gerg watching her smile.

"You are not alone," Gerg speculated.

"I am."

"You will not trick me," the dwarf growled, looking up into the trees. He lifted his pike and when he did, Roberta pulled the hatchet from the belt. "You will die another day," Gerg said – then turned and vanished in the underbrush.

Roberta pulled the root from the earth, calmly took the filled basket and walked back to the house. All the while the hatchet remained in her hands. She knew that her fingers were shaking, but just barely. To anyone watching her she looked in control, in command of her faculties, still the mighty Archer she had once been. She had been able to fool Gerg. She would never be that lucky again.

By the time Lily, Andrew and the children were up, Roberta had prepared and swallowed the remedies. She felt stronger and, looking in the mirror, she could see that she looked a shade healthier, too. She kept her early morning meeting with Gerg to herself. The children didn't need to know everything. They were in high spirits after their latest adventures – and they couldn't wait to finally meet the lord. When Andrew suggested taking the car, Roberta balked at the idea.

"We'll walk," Roberta said resolutely – and so they walked.

Andrew had taken the path before, together with Lily. For the children, it was their first visit to Oakham Park. They followed Witney Road past the cemetery, then left

Finstock and continued on along Charlbury Road. Just before crossing the bridge across the River Evenlode, they took the foot path along the river that would lead them along the edges of Oakham Park to the main gate.

Andrew and Lily were trailing Roberta and the children as Lily seemed to want to stop at just about every flower, bush and leaf of grass. Roberta didn't mind, the time had been set aside for all such eventualities.

"So Dad is part selkie?" Ellie asked Roberta with a glance back to where Andrew stood. While Lily pulled leaves from bushes and ate them, he stood there, holding her hand, his glance seemingly lost in the flow of the river.

"Well, Corisander certainly seems to have that notion," Roberta replied. "And it certainly would explain the rare gifts you've been given. You might be the only humans in the world whose parents both carry the blood of fairy beings within them."

"Dad does go swimming every day when we're in New York," Milo said.

"And he goes white in the face when he hasn't had water for a while," Ellie added.

"Selkie people," Nick said, shaking his head. "What next?"

"Well, I do have a dragon uncle," Roberta mentioned evenly.

When she saw the look on their faces, she burst out laughing.

"What did I miss?" Andrew asked, catching up with them.

"We were just talking about seals and dragons," Roberta said, smiling. "Your children have a vivid imagination, Andrew."

"My genes," Andrew proclaimed proudly.

As they walked along the narrow river, Roberta told them that the rolling hills around the river valley had been Tolkien's inspiration for the Shire, the land of the hobbits.

"Did hobbits exist?" Milo asked. Nick gave him a light shove and tilted his head in the direction of their father.

"Their existence is about as real as that of dwarves and elves," Roberta said, with a wink at them both.

"Did hobbits exist?" Andrew said, imitating Milo, then added with a grin, "Seriously, guys, maybe some of you need to lay off those fantasy books for a while."

The skies darkened as they slowly continued on the footpath and soon they reached the corner post of the estate's fenced off park. The fence was high and solid, the same one that circumvented all of Wychwood. Through the meshed wire, they saw open meadows and clusters of old trees and in between them, hundreds of deer.

"Amazing, aren't they?" Andrew asked. "There's just such a powerful sense of tranquility about these creatures, don't you think?"

"Yes," Milo said.

Roberta knew that there were roughly five hundred deer, free to roam from the park to the forest as they pleased. The deer were dozing and grazing, some of them entirely ignoring the humans watching them, others alert to the tips of their ears. One large herd seemed bored, standing in a cluster. Another herd charged across the meadow with wild abandon and disappeared from sight behind Oakham Park House. In the distance, the imposing building seemed far from impressive.

"Guys, look," Andrew said, pointing at a stag not far from where they stood. The stag came closer, staring at all of them - not stopping until its nose almost touched the fence. "Amazing," Andrew whispered. He rummaged through his pockets, found his phone and readied to take a picture. It was then that the stag hurled a deafening bellow at them. The children stood their ground while Andrew fumbled and dropped his phone. "Jesus," he muttered, his hands shaking.

"Let's move on," Roberta said. "Wouldn't want to be late, would we?"

She kept noticing the strange behavior of animals. Just that morning, before her encounter with Gerg, she had seen a flock of birds chirping loudly and chasing each other from tree to tree. Then they had suddenly huddled at the center of a beech and fallen absolutely silent. The odd bellowing of the stag wasn't nearly as eerie as the silence of the birds had been.

Roberta ushered Andrew, Lily and the children on and five minutes later they arrived at the gates to the estate where an emerald green minibus was waiting for them. The gates receded silently. They stepped in and onto the minibus where an elderly liveried chauffeur greeted them curtly. A short ride later he delivered them to the stairs of Oakham Park House. Standing right in front of the house, it always felt monumental to Roberta with its thirty large windows on walls that stretched far in either direction.

"Roberta," Lord Francis Thornton said. "It is so nice to see you."

He was all elegance as he walked down the steps to greet them. Impeccably dressed, he carried himself with quiet dignity. There were two things that made his overall appearance more than the cliché of a nobleman. The first thing was his hair. While his white beard was cropped neatly, his white hair was shoulder long and flowing freely. The second thing was his leg, but the children would only find out later about that particular peculiarity. For the moment, all they noticed was that the old man walked with a cane.

Roberta playfully curtseyed before shaking hands with her old friend. As he shook one hand after the other, Roberta did the introductions.

"May I introduce Lord Thornton. Francis, you remember Lily," she began. Lily acknowledged neither the people nor the many deer grazing nearby. She seemed mesmerized by the emerald green meadows.

"She's not better, I see," he said with genuine concern.

"Oh, I don't know, there have been improvements," Andrew replied, shaking Lord Thornton's hand. "Andrew Murphy. It's a pleasure to meet you, Sir."

"Please, none of that Sir this and Lord that. Do me the kindness of calling me Francis. And that of course goes for all of you," he said, looking at the children.

"These are Nick, Milo and Ellie," Roberta said.

"Ah yes, the young Archers," Thornton said.

"Murphys," Roberta corrected.

"Of course," Thornton said. "Please, follow me. I believe lunch is served."

Francis was a masterful conversationalist. The topic didn't matter, his insights and a voice like velvet had always made Roberta smile. She smiled now as he showed the Murphys to the dining room where the long table, beautifully set, was beckoning them. They were served course after course and through it all Francis asked questions about the life of a journalist, the health of Lily, the hobbies and plans of the children. Roberta had not told him about her impending demise and hoped it wouldn't come up.

"I don't know," Milo said with a shrug.

"Nothing? No hobbies? Nothing you particularly like, young man?" Francis asked.

"Well … I like … stories, I guess," Milo said.

"Ah, stories," Francis said with a wink in Roberta's direction. "These might not by any chance be fantasy stories, tales, legends, mythology, that sort of thing?"

"Yes," Milo said.

"I've always been intensely interested in the very same thing. It's why I've become a historian, in fact. History is, after all, just that – stories upon stories. And the more closely you look at the tales told for as long as people remember, the more truth you find," Francis explained and only Andrew did not know what he was talking about.

"Roberta has this wonderful library," Andrew

interjected. "The kids are practically devouring her books."

"I do know that library," Francis replied with a smile at Roberta. "Roberta's family has collected quite some rarities over the years."

"Nothing compared to what Francis has," Roberta said, returning the compliment. "Mind you – his library is bigger than our house."

"You're exaggerating, my dear … if only slightly."

When dessert had been served, Francis took them all into the library. Roberta knew that the children would not be disappointed. She herself had been in that room many times, talking to Francis, often into the night, about lives lost, saved and lived.

The library of Oakham Park House had none of what one usually saw in the homes of nobility. This was not a place to smoke cigars and sip brandy in polished leather chairs, this was a place of study, a place of learning. Built two floors high, the library was walled by bookshelves everywhere. Spiral staircases on either side led to an upper walkway. Chairs and sofas invited for discussion and a large desk was overflowing with books and notes and maps, with some of them spilling onto the rugs around the desk.

"Bit of a mess, I'm afraid," Francis said apologetically.

Roberta observed the children closely and was not surprised to see Nick instantly scanning the large room. A moment later he walked to a shelf that looked like all others. There it was, the same ornamented leaf that had activated the secret shelf in their house. Before pushing it, he turned to Francis.

"We have the same at our house," Nick said.

"And I'm sure you'd like to see what's behind this one, wouldn't you?" Francis said with a twinkle in his eyes. "Go ahead, young man."

Nick pushed the button and both Milo and Ellie moved in closer to see what the shelf behind the shelf would reveal. What they discovered were a series of wrapped first-edition comic books.

"Aren't they wonderful?"

Andrew seemed more excited than the children and glowed when Francis mentioned that he'd be most welcome to leaf through a pristine original Action Comics No. 1, the comic that had introduced Superman in 1938. For a while, the children roamed from shelf to shelf, explored the upper landing as well and pointed out books to each other. And for a while, Francis and Roberta just sat on the sofa and allowed Andrew to enjoy one comic after another. Lily sat on the lush old carpet in front of them, her fingers tracing ornaments woven in Persia in centuries past.

"You'd think those weavers knew about the flow, wouldn't you?" Francis suggested quietly enough for Andrew not to hear.

"The flow, frozen in time," Roberta mused.

"I'm quite glad it is, Roberta," Francis said. "I might go mad if the rug were changing all the time."

"We would all go mad in the flow," Roberta added evenly. "Just as they did because of our constant clamor.

What do you think, Francis, shall we?"

Francis nodded. He leaned on his cane and rose. Walking to Andrew, he told him about the flower room and the extensive gardens he could explore with Lily. It was with much reluctance that Andrew returned the comics to their shelves. Together with Lily, he left the library. Francis watched them walk down the hallway, gave him another friendly wave and then closed the library doors.

CHAPTER TWENTY-EIGHT

THE ROLLRIGHT STONES

"Well then, young Archers, welcome to Wychwood," Francis said as he turned. "Your grandmother has already told me about your first exploits. You seem to be quite talented."

Nick, Milo and Ellie came to stand next to each other, uncertain about the man in front of them, wondering what they were doing here. Roberta, still sitting on the sofa, smiled.

"There are no secrets here," she said. "Francis knows everything I know … and sometimes he knows more. Tell them about magic, Francis."

"Nick," Francis said. "Take another look at the shelf."

Nick frowned. He went back to the first edition comic books and soon found another leaf. Pressing on the ornament, a third shelf was revealed behind the comic books. Fascinated, the children approached and discovered old books, folders and binders, handwritten scrolls and rows of research diaries.

"What is all this?" Ellie asked.

"My life's work," Francis explained. "While the Archers 'protect the forest and those who roam within', my aim is, and has always been, the destruction of the dome."

Moments later, Francis was sitting next to Roberta again,

the children in chairs opposite them, leaning forward, frowning.

"Does O'Rein know about your work?" Nick asked.

"I've never told him," Roberta said in Francis' stead. "Francis has discovered much in his life, but so far nothing that would help break the spell of the dome. And unless that happens, I would not want to raise hope with O'Rein and the others."

"Raise hope? If the dome's gone, wouldn't they die?" Ellie asked.

"Without the dome, all creatures would be exposed to time. That is the way of the world. Everything has its time."

"How can you want them to die?" Milo asked angrily.

"They don't want to live forever," Roberta replied.

"Their time was over thousands of years ago, Milo," Francis explained.

Milo looked from one to the other and the more sense they made, the angrier he became.

"But it's Wychwood," Milo said. "We're Archers. We're like the elves. We're elfish ourselves. We're – we're – that's our family in there!"

"You are absolutely right, Milo," Francis said serenely. "The choice is theirs, will be theirs. But for now there is no choice to be made. The dome remains. I have become a historian for this reason and this reason only, to find a way to reverse the spell."

"They elves would grow old and die … as we do," Roberta said.

"I … I don't want that," Ellie said, tears in her eyes.

"And I don't want redcaps running around killing people," Milo added. He was still furious, pacing around the library. But Roberta could see him slowing down, thinking, realizing that either way would lead to death. For Roberta and Francis, the way was clear because both of them had seen too much violent death in their lifetimes.

"You must have found something," Nick said.

"I have indeed," Francis replied. "I have found charlatans and make-believe in every part of the world. But I have also found places where the flow remains strong. I have found proof that magic still remains."

"Can you do magic?" Ellie asked, interrupting him.

"I wish," Francis said with a thunderous laugh. "Magic spells were performed by the mages of old, powerful beings like Andill who made the dome. I hope to one day find the spell that breaks the spell … but only one such as O'Rein the Wise can use it. As I have said, the choice will be theirs."

"Good," Milo grumbled.

"I have found many things but when it comes to the dome, there has been little I have been able to make sense of," Francis continued. "Pieced together from local tales, ancient ballads and bardic poems I have come to believe that there are three things that must be found in three places by three people … You can imagine my interest when I found out about the three of you. My sincere hope is that you are these three people."

"Tell them about the Rollright Stones, Francis," Roberta

said. She was sitting back, comfortably nestled into the sofa and watching the children, their faces, their reactions. Even if they couldn't yet fully comprehend the magnitude of what they were hearing, they seemed to feel it in their hearts.

"Not far from here there is a group of stones," he began. "Neolithic, they say. The stone circle is called the 'King's Men'. At a distance from the circle stands a solitary rock, the 'King Stone'. Legend has it that those stones were once men." He paused, then turned to Roberta with a mischievous smile. "Do the witch, Roberta, go on."

"It's an old rhyme about a king who wanted to conquer all of England and a witch who said he would – if he could see beyond a hill by taking no more than seven steps," Roberta said. She leaned forward and continued in the ominously grating voice of a witch.

"Seven long strides thou shalt take, says she, and if Long Compton thou canst see, King of England thou shalt be."

"When they heard the words of the witch, the men gathered in a circle to discuss it," Francis said. "But the king didn't wait. He thought he could do it, took seven strides but failed to reach the top of the hill to see beyond it."

"As Long Compton thou canst not see," Roberta continued in the witch's voice, "King of England thou shalt not be. Rise up stick and stand still stone, for King of England thou shalt be none. Thou and thy men hoar stones shall be, and I myself an elder tree."

For a moment there, the children were looking at her as

if she really were a witch, Roberta thought and smiled. Then she leaned back in the sofa and Francis took over once more.

"Just a fairytale, of course," Francis said. "But as you three know by now, there's often truth to fairytales. In this case, I've come to believe that the 'King Stone' is none other than Andill himself, the mage who cast the spell."

Francis went on to tell them that, pieced together from tales going back to ancient scrolls, the place of the Rollright Stones seemed indeed to be one of the three places where one of the three ingredients for the spell to remove the dome would be found. He had been there dozens of times and had found nothing.

"I hope that you will be more successful," he said to the children.

"I want to see the stones," Ellie said.

"And you will," Roberta said. "We will visit them together."

"What about the other places?" Nick asked.

"I believe that one is a well. Unfortunately, there are countless wells. But as difficult as that is, I'm afraid the third place poses a far greater challenge. It seems that the third place is a tree."

The children readily agreed to help Francis if he thought they might be of use. Roberta saw them glancing at each other, gazing across the library as they listened to Francis. Their world was expanding with every new sentence spoken. Finally, Francis paused.

"Shall we go see what your parents are up to?" he asked.

The children nodded. "Nick, would you mind closing the shelf again?"

"Grandma mentioned that you've known each other since you were kids," Nick said while pushing the shelf closed. With a click the lock snapped into the place and the first edition comic books were on display again. "How long have you known about ... you know, everything?"

"I've known since I was ten years old," Francis said, glancing at Roberta. She knew that, what he was about to reveal, would always weigh heaviest on him.

"It was the day I met your grandmother for the first time," Francis continued and squeezed her hand. "And the day she saved my life. My brother Albert and I chose to ignore our parents' warnings that day. We knew to never enter Wychwood. When we did, we were met by three redcaps. They killed Albert on the spot," Francis said, the words coming out faster now. "I was in shock, of course. They laughed and let me run and ran after me. I made it almost to the edge of the forest when they blocked my way out. It was then that Roberta and her brother Chester appeared and fought the redcaps. They killed two of them and I ran on, but I didn't know that you should never run in a straight line. The third of the redcaps threw his axe and it ... well ..."

Francis pushed against the sides of his right leg just below the knee. There was a light clicking sound. With that, Francis pulled an artificial limb from his pant leg. Roberta had seen this before but it still looked strangely funny to her. Francis was holding up half a leg that was within a striped sock and an elegant leather shoe.

Andrew opened the door to the library at that exact moment. One hand on the door, the other holding on to Lily, he gaped at the sight.

"You enjoyed the gardens, I hope?" Francis asked casually as if he were not holding a prosthetic in his hand.

"Yes, wonderful," Andrew said, looking at the leg. "What is …?"

"Oh, we were merely swapping a few stories," Francis said as he pushed the prosthetic back in place, took his cane and rose. "Look at the time. Please do join me for tea."

Late that night Roberta would tell her grandchildren the rest of the story. How she and Chester had beaten back the third redcap long enough for Francis to crawl out of Wychwood. He had almost bled to death that day and his parents attributed the story of monsters in the forest to his state of shock. But Albert was missing and so was one half of Francis' right leg. Search and hunting parties were organized, consisting of people unburdened by the apprehensions of the locals. The search for a maniacal child abductor began and the forest was combed for months without result. In time, the story of the missing Albert Thornton and his brother Francis became yet another tale of Wychwood.

CHAPTER TWENTY-NINE

TO MAKE
AN ELF APPEAR

Corisander mused about a stone circle, a well and a tree. He had heard the stories of Andill being devastated by what he had done to those forever trapped within the forest. He had done it because he knew that there was no stopping humans. Humanity would rise and conquer everything. Some said that Andill had turned himself and his men to stone.

The children had met in Nick's room and had talked about Lord Francis Thornton and everything he had told them long into the night. Corisander had been there with them, listening, wondering. The children might indeed be the ones, but even if they could destroy the dome, Corisander was far from sure whether that should ever happen. Of the many creatures imprisoned in the forest, how many were truly gone? Just a few days earlier a spirit had reached out for them. It seemed forgotten for now, by the children, by Roberta. As if that night really had been nothing but a dream.

All Corisander could do was to keep his senses open to the forest.

Roberta had wanted to wake up the Archer within them

– and she had succeeded in doing so. And the visit to Lord Francis Thornton had only fueled their already heightened interests. The next morning the children left the house early and were back before nine, carrying a large shopping bag. Corisander followed them to the shed.

"This is never going to work," Nick argued.

"How do you know? It might," Milo replied.

"I like the idea," Ellie said.

Corisander watched them climb the tree behind the shed. The leaves covered most of what was up there, but a cat's eyes were often pretty useful. The children placed the bag high up in the tree where several large branches created a comfortable lounging area. Ellie produced a ball of string and scissors and with it they began hanging up everything they had bought at the shop, small bags of potato chips and various assortments of sweets as well as a dozen chocolate bars. When they were done, the area looked as if it had been decorated for a party.

"The lady in the shop thought we were nuts." Milo grinned.

"I think she mumbled something about crazy Americans," Ellie added.

"That's exactly what we are," Nick said as he and Milo began to pierce and tear the wrappers of everything that was hanging now.

Pretty clever, Corisander thought as he realized what they were up to. Tracking the elves was impossible, finding Bromley was difficult. But one like Anthor might find the scent of the hanging treasures irresistible and would come to visit them here. All they had to do was wait in the safety of the tree.

"And if Anthor shows up, we'll ask him to get O'Rein," Milo suggested.

"Maybe O'Rein doesn't know about Andill and the Rollright Stones," Ellie mused as she found a comfortable place to sit.

"Maybe he does. Worth asking," Milo replied.

"Definitely," Nick agreed. "So where are we today? Please tell me we didn't go back to the petting zoo. You should have seen the way Dad looked at me."

"We've gone to the Leafield village fair," Ellie explained.

"Did we walk?" Nick asked.

"We took the old bicycles," Milo explained. "Grandma's hidden them behind the house."

"We're getting good at this," Nick mentioned.

"Lying to Dad?" Ellie asked uneasily.

"Yeah," Nick replied.

Corisander felt the mood in the tree drift into an uncomfortable silence.

"We should tell him," Ellie finally said.

"We can't," Milo shot at her. "We promised Grandma."

"Ellie," Nick cautioned. "If Dad knew about this, any of this, he would take us away from here in a heartbeat."

Ellie sat there, pensive, but eventually nodded and leaned back against the tree. Milo brought up Lord Thornton again, Francis to them. They talked about fabulous Oakham Park House, the food, the library, the legend of the Rollright Stones and the story of Andill. And they discussed animatedly the prosthetic leg and Dad walking in just then. They agreed that they all very much liked the old man.

"Maybe we should shut up for a while," Nick suggested.

The others nodded and Corisander heard no more for a while. Lying there in the grass, he watched Lily and Andrew step out of the house. She sat down in the grass, rolled onto her back and Andrew joined her. Together they watched clouds slowly cross the sky, with Andrew narrating their shapes and busting them into new ones.

Corisander knew that the children were watching this from their hiding place and he didn't need to see their faces to know that they were smiling.

Three hours later, Andrew had taken Lily for a walk, the children were still sitting in the tree, their backs aching, their minds bored. Milo was softly snoring and Nick kicked his foot.

"What?" Milo mumbled.

"Like I said, this is never going to work," Nick said.

"We could do some training," Ellie suggested, then added with a mischievous grin. "You need all the training you can get."

Corisander heard them laugh and egg each other on and he saw Roberta standing on the patio, her hands around a cup of Roberta Kibble's Famous Pain Relief Tea. He knew that the old woman was suffering but she wouldn't let it show. Instead she used her life-long herbal learnings to keep the smile in place. One day soon those eyes would never open again. Corisander wasn't looking forward to that day. He would greatly miss her. Roberta smiled as she heard the voices up in the tree, as she watched them jump down.

"I'm going to show them a few moves," Ellie called to her grandmother, laughing out loud as Nick playfully kicked her. Milo and Nick chased Ellie into the shed and they emerged again, moments later, suited up.

"Be careful," Roberta called and waved as they jumped into the nearest tree. "And stay together, young Archers!"

Corisander watched them wave and vanish into the green.

The things Ellie could do were impossible and continuously frustrating for the boys. The gift of the Air allowed her to barely touch branches before vaulting off again and sometimes she was able to sail through the air twice as far as they could. Where trees were too far apart, Nick and Milo used the ground-leap, a quick jump to and run on the forest floor before ascending again. Ellie would simply swing and sail across such clearings.

Nick was nowhere near as good as Ellie, but had the benefit of the Eye. Invariably he chose the perfect path for what would work for him and that allowed him to keep chasing Ellie and bypassing Milo. They chased each other, tried to incorporate some of what Ellie showed them, then chased each other some more.

Finally, they decided it was time to head back to the food-decorated tree – they were all anxious to see whether their offerings had enticed a certain elf.

CHAPTER THIRTY

THE MAZE OF SKULLS

They lined up on a high branch of a gnarly old oak near Newhill Plain. Ellie looked at Nick, eyes flashing with the excitement of another race.

"First one back gets –" Ellie began when Nick already jumped.

"See you there!" Nick shouted and was off. Feigning indignation at first, Ellie broke out laughing and chased after Nick.

Milo just shrugged. He knew he'd be third and didn't much care. Milo swung his rope and followed them. He sensed squirrels nearby, a fox below, a few deer up ahead. Milo noticed that his sense of direction was getting better every day. He now recognized individual trees that would have looked all the same to him before.

When Milo sensed a human being in the forest below, he stopped. There was no way of alerting the others and so he decided to just wait out whoever was passing down there. Milo recognized him instantly, it was the man from the farm across the street, Gordon Cowley. He had a rucksack on his back and a bow in his hand as he stealthily followed a deer trail. "Stay together," Grandma had urged. Milo smirked. It was too late for that – if he went off to get them, the man down there might die. "Protectors of the forest and those who roam within," Milo whispered to himself and followed the farmer.

Cowley was poaching, an offense Robert the Archer would have killed him for on the spot. Milo watched him duck down to a snare. He removed a dead hare, then set the trap again. With the carcass stuffed into his rucksack, Cowley placed an arrow on his bow and continued on the track in silence. With every step he avoided twigs that might alert his prey. Milo had no doubt that, just like Christopher Smith, Cowley had been the prey himself many times. Milo made a mental note of the trees and bushes – planning to return later to remove the snare.

Milo sensed Wychwood teeming with wildlife but none of it showed itself to Cowley. He had no idea what he should do if something happened. Well, most likely Ellie and Nick would backtrack any moment now.

He was just wondering what he should do if Cowley were to shoot a deer — when the ambush happened. It was so fast that neither Cowley nor Milo had a chance to react.

Three redcaps, all carrying their pikes, attacked Cowley simultaneously. In a flash, Milo realized that they had been waiting in their stone-like squatting position. It apparently made them invisible to Milo's senses. Milo recognized Caark who rushed forward and knocked Cowley unconscious with the back of his axe. The second dwarf was Urk. With his hook he pulled open a hatch in the forest floor. The third dwarf, taller than the others, gave Cowley a kick and tossed him down into the hole. A second later they were all inside and the trap door was shut once more.

The attack had taken no more than five seconds.

Milo blinked. It was as if nothing had happened. Cowley was gone, there was no sign of a hatch, just the forest floor with the same plants and leaves and roots as before.

Frantic, Milo looked around, sensed around. If he waited for Nick and Ellie, Cowley would be dead. If he went to get them, Cowley would be dead. The elves would have prevented this from happening, Milo thought in frustration. Maybe Cowley was already dead. Milo shook his head angrily and maybe he was shaking off his fear. He had to do something.

Milo jumped and landed softly on the ground. He frantically searched for the hatch. When he found it, he managed to hook his fingers into a crack. I need the Rage, he thought and as he thought it, he felt it rise. Milo pried open the heavy hatch, breaking the lock in the progress. He stepped back hurriedly, knife in hand, expecting one of the redcaps to jump out at him. When nothing happened, Milo moved forward and looked into a shaft where a ladder led down into pitch-black darkness.

He looked around once more, hoping for Nick or Ellie or the elves to appear but he was alone and remained alone and every moment of waiting increased the chances of Cowley's death. Taking a deep breath, Milo climbed down the ladder. The vertical shaft seemed to go on for a long time, then he stood inside a tunnel that led in two opposite directions. To his surprise it wasn't dark down here. Oil lamps, fixed to the walls at regular intervals, cast circles of yellow light.

The tunnel was far from just a hole dug in the earth. It appeared to have been built over the course of many years, with well-hewn stone slabs that covered the ground, the walls and the ceilings. The walls contained alcove after alcove and every one of them contained a skull. There were animal skulls and human skulls and Milo wondered if one of them might be Chester. There was also elongated miniature skulls and giant-sized skulls and for a moment Milo felt that all of those empty eye sockets were staring at him.

An annoyed grunt echoed through the tunnel from the left and reminded Milo of Cowley. He hurried off, as quietly as he could, in that direction. Milo stopped at every corner, waited, listened, then ran again past countless skulls.

When he heard voices, Milo slowed and cautiously looked around the next corner. There they were, walking next to each other, completely at ease as if they were out for a stroll. Caark walked on the left, the pike over his shoulder. The tall dwarf was in the middle, using his pike like a walking staff. And Urk had Cowley flung over his shoulder, while dragging his pike along the side.

"Tonk will be pleased, Taar," Urk said.

"No doubt," the tall dwarf named Taar replied.

"This head is mine," Caark argued. "I've hunted this one for a long time and it was my idea to be there today. This one's mine," he said again, slapping Cowley's head.

Taar suddenly and violently turned and slammed Caark against the wall.

"Tonk decides who gets to take the head," Taar said, spitting the words into Caark's face. "If you don't like it, he will take your head as well."

Furious, Caark pushed back and slammed Taar against the other wall. Urk had just enough time to get out of the way.

"How about I take yours?" Caark screamed at Taar. He suddenly pushed himself off, then stabbed at Taar with his pike. Taar blocked with his own pike. Milo watched in amazement as they went at each other in a fight to the death with pikes, axes and knives. As they pushed, kicked, blocked and attacked, Urk stepped further away from them. When Caark and Taar slashed the air and the walls with their weapons, sparks flew. Urk took another step away from them, Cowley still over his shoulder … and every step back took him closer to the corner where Milo was standing.

Milo saw a chance when Taar threw a knife that buried itself in Caark's arm. He tore it out again and hurled it away before launching himself at Taar once more. The flying knife almost hit Urk, causing him to take another step back. Milo stepped out, tripped the surprised Urk and yanked him around the corner. Urk tried to yell but Milo smashed a massive skull down on his head and hit him three times until Urk stopped moving.

As the fight continued on the other side of the corner, Milo grabbed the still unconscious Cowley by his rucksack and pulled him back to where he had come from. Milo yanked and pulled and rushed as fast as he could when he realized two things, one was that the fighting noises had stopped, the other that Cowley was coming to.

"Get up," Milo snapped at Cowley. "Come on, get up!"

Dazed, Cowley looked up at him, looked around, then stumbled to his feet.

"What is – where am – who are you?"

Milo pushed him, Cowley stumbled. Milo pushed him forward again.

"Run or we're both going to die!"

Confused and frowning, the man was awake enough now to realize that the fear in the boy's eyes was very real. This and being in a tunnel filled with skulls was enough to get him to start running. Milo instinctively knew his way back through the maze of tunnels, certain that he would find the way out.

When he saw the shaft of light up ahead, he grabbed Cowley and pushed him to the ladder. Behind them, footsteps were storming in their direction.

"Climb, climb, climb already!" Milo shouted at Cowley.

"Where's my bow?" Cowley asked, still half dazed.

"Climb!"

Looking back to where they had come from, Cowley saw something he couldn't comprehend. Three nightmarish creatures were charging toward him. He scrambled up the ladder as fast as he could.

Milo was right behind Cowley, saw the light coming closer but at the same time heard the footsteps and curses of the redcaps far too close for comfort. Cowley missed a rung, grabbed hold again and kept going.

"Move!" Milo cried, terrified now.

They were halfway up the shaft when Milo felt a hand on his foot. He glared down and saw Caark staring up at him, eyes blazing with fury.

"You!" he screamed.

Milo hooked into the ladder with one arm. His free hand reached for the crossbow on his back. Cowley was almost at the top, he would make it. Milo aimed for Caark's head and shot. The dwarf moved his head just in time but howled as the arrow stuck in his shoulder. It just seemed to make him more determined.

"You're still mine," Caark snarled. "Shoot ten of your arrows – Caark will not let go."

In his terror, Milo summoned the Rage. He threw the crossbow at Caark's face then began to climb once more, pulling with him the whole of Caark's weight. One rung, then another. Caark was dangling, incredulous but, if anything, even angrier than before … then suddenly the weight of Caark was gone. The dwarf had let go. Milo looked down into the tunnel and saw the three dwarves staring up – but not at him.

When Milo looked up, there stood Culanxan, still as a statue. His bow was extended, the arrow pointing past Milo into the tunnel. He appeared utterly calm.

"Move," he said to Milo.

Milo did as he was told and hurried up onto the forest floor. Cowley was flat on the ground, eyes closed, his face blank. Milo saw traces of powder. Culanxan relaxed his bow and placed the arrow back in his quiver. Milo glanced down into the tunnel once more. Only Caark was left standing there.

"You were lucky twice," Caark called up. "You will not be lucky a third –" That was the last they heard of Caark as Culanxan had kicked the hatch shut. The elf turned and evenly looked at Milo.

"I'm sorry," Milo said. "But you guys can't be everywhere and when they dragged him down, I mean, what was I supposed to do?"

Then the bald elf did something Milo would never forget. He smiled.

"There are poems and songs about my deeds," Culanxan said. "Some are fanciful, most are true. But I have never wandered down into the realm of the redcaps to save a life. You have done well. And one day they may sing your praises."

For Milo, the journey back to the edge of the forest was like a dream. He was in the company of Culanxan and watched in awe as he effortlessly jumped from tree to tree with Cowley over his shoulder. They were close to the fence when they came across Nick and Ellie, both of them frantic and exhausted.

"We've been looking everywhere for you!" Ellie said.

"We were supposed to stay together," Nick add, smacking Milo.

It was only then that they she saw Culanxan.

"What's going on?" Ellie asked, frowning.

"Your brother will tell you. I will inform the others of what you have achieved today, Milo. If not his friendship, you will have Shendak's respect. As a gift, take this."

He handed Milo a fist-sized leather pouch and Milo didn't know what to say. He smiled. Culanxan jumped to a tree on the edge of the forest and lowered the unconscious farmer to the ground outside the fence. His work done, he nodded at the children and jumped. They strained their ears to hear Culanxan move through the trees but there was nothing. Just the sounds of the birds and a gentle wind in the crowns of the trees. Milo proceeded to tell them about everything that had occurred.

"That was stupid," Ellie exclaimed angrily.

"I know," Milo agreed. "But I'm fine – and Cowley is alive."

"No more races," Nick demanded. "No more games. Whatever we do, we do together. Okay?"

Both Milo and Ellie nodded.

"What did he give you?" Ellie asked, pointing at the pouch in Milo's hand.

Milo opened it eagerly and discovered that it was filled with the blue powder.

"It's the memory-erasing powder."

"Cool, might come in handy," Nick said. "Now one more thing. Just so we're clear. If the elves are ever going to be singing any songs in the future, I better be in them, too."

When they went back to the tree they had decorated with gifts for Anthor, they discovered that only the empty strings were still there, moving lightly with the wind. It appeared that their method had worked. They laughed, imagining Anthor showing up, discovering the hanging treasures and jumping from one to the other, salivating.

"Let's try this again," Nick said.

CHAPTER THIRTY-ONE

THE OLD KING

Children of elves and selkies.

Once there had been no such thing. The idea of mating with humans had not existed. It had been beyond imagination. Apparently, things had changed. The Old King did not harbor any ill will towards any of them. He understood love. He had felt it and he was beginning to feel it again.

He was glad, in fact. Glad that a Wychwood elf had fallen in love with one of the Archers he had heard so much about these past days. And he was glad that the younglings' father existed because there once had been the love of a selkie in his family's past. Without love, the younglings would not be here. Without love, the Old King would be imprisoned forever in this place.

He had begun to reflect on his situation … and he had begun to curse Andill, he who was responsible for the abominable dome that kept the Old King.

He had rested. He had waited. He had gathered strength and soon he would be rid of the dome.

The younglings would help.

Then the younglings would die.

And the Old King rose.

CHAPTER THIRTY-TWO

THE SOUND
OF WYCHWOOD MUSIC

Nick, Milo and Ellie were at their politest as they ransacked the village shop for the second time in one day. It was early afternoon and the episode in the tunnel of the redcaps seemed in the distant past.

Shop manager Harriet Thorne couldn't believe her eyes when the "crazy Americans" were there again, this time filling two bags with everything sweet and salty.

"Who are you?" she asked suspiciously.

"Roberta Kibble is our grandmother," Ellie replied with a polite smile.

"My goodness," Harriet Thorne gasped, taking an involuntary step back. "I should have known. You're Archers."

"Anything wrong with that?" Milo asked roughly.

"No, course not. Please do give your grandmother my regards."

Nick paid and pocketed the change. At the door, he turned.

"It's all true, you know," he offered in the hushed voice of conspiracy.

"What is?" Harriet Thorne asked.

"Everything," Nick replied, drawing out the word. With that he pushed the others out of the shop. "The crazy Americans will be back," he said as the door closed.

Once outside the shop they laughed out loud and as they walked back, their laughter erupted again every time they remembered Harriet Thorne's flustered face. They passed church and cemetery and soon came upon Christopher Smith's house.

The old man rigidly stood by the drystone wall that separated his garden from the street. He stared at the children, then waved them over to his side. Together they crossed the street and stopped by the waist high wall.

"I remember you," Smith mused.

"You do?" Nick asked. Just like the others, he wondered whether the memory-erasing powder might not have worked on Smith.

"Yes, I talked to you the other day. I told you about the monsters. I told you to stay out of Wychwood. Did you stay out of Wychwood?"

"Of course," Milo replied casually. "Besides, we're from New York. We couldn't care less about trees and stuff."

"… Good, that's good," Smith muttered and stared at them again. "I just … thought I saw you somewhere in a forest."

"Why? Do you go into the forest?" Ellie asked innocently.

"No. I don't think so. I'm not sure. I want to but every time I do I wake up outside the fence. I am … I …," Smith lost his train of thought and looked past them to where

Wychwood stood in awesome silence.

"Mr. Smith," Nick asked. "What are all of these sculptures?"

To the children, it was quite obvious that they were interpretations of the redcaps the elves had saved him from many times.

"They are nightmares. My nightmares," Smith explained, then focused again. "I told you about the monsters. Don't believe me, but there's proof. Go to pub and see for yourself."

"I think we're a bit too young for that," Nick said amiably.

"Not that," Smith said, frustrated. "Not drinking. Looking. You're supposed to look. Have you ever heard of the Dunsdon Brothers? Tom, Dick and Harry?"

"Seriously? Tom, Dick and Harry?" Nick asked.

"Yes, seriously. Very seriously. They were the original Tom, Dick and Harry, in fact. These brothers were poachers and even your ancestors could not catch them."

"Can't be a true story then," Milo said smugly.

"The Dunsdon Brothers," Smith continued, glowering at Milo, "readied to go about their business one day and Tom was first to enter Wychwood. As the others still reached for their bows and arrows, they heard a scream from within the woods."

For the moment the bags in their hands were forgotten, Anthor would have to wait. Listening to the old man, the children leaned forward.

"Dick, always the cautious one, gave Harry a push to go

217

and check," Smith continued. "But even before Harry Dunsdon took one single step into Wychwood forest, his brother Tom came back out. He was walking with big steps, straight as an arrow and there was no head on his neck. Dick and Harry screamed and screamed and all the while Tom walked in a direct line to the pub. When he realized that he could neither order nor drink a pint, he died. The blood stain is there to this day. You go see for yourself. Now, did Dick and Harry ever go back into Wychwood after that? No, they did not. I see you looking at the forest," he added, glaring at them. "Now you go and you remember Tom Dunsdon, Children – and don't say I didn't warn you!"

As they walked home they wondered how many other Tales of Wychwood were floating around in the world. They knew one thing, at least half of the story of Tom, Dick and Harry Dunsdon was very likely true.

It was dark outside, long after dinner, when Roberta finally had the chance to catch up with the children about their day's adventures. Andrew and Lily were upstairs, with Lily engrossed in the wooden ceiling of the library and all the leaves and flowers one of her ancestors had carved in it. Andrew was quickly developing an interest in the world of selkies and read stories out loud so that Lily could hear them, too … just in case.

Roberta sat in her usual chair and Ellie, sitting next to her, was playing one of the flutes she had found upstairs. In the light streaming from the windows, Nick twirled a knife. He kept throwing it up and catching it again as

Roberta had done just a few days ago. Nick seemed different, they all seemed different. How could they not be? Their world had been taken from them and replaced with another that was full of peril. Roberta felt guilty because this was exactly what she had hoped for.

Milo sat at Ellie's feet, listening to the ever-changing flow of her melodies, his eyes on the forest that was little more than a obscure wall beyond the fence. The boy had told her about his rescue of Gordon Cowley and she found it surprising that he was still awake. She remembered those days of life and death. She remembered that she had always slept wonderfully after the intensity of such days.

"Tell me about the tunnels," Roberta asked.

"They were … actually kind of nice. It was more like being in a castle than underground."

"Do you think you could go down there again?" Roberta knew that she was asking too much. She knew that it didn't make sense and yet she also knew that the return of her brother's skull was her final wish.

"No," Ellie said instead of Milo. With the mellow sounds of the flute gone, the evening suddenly seemed to have cooled.

"Whatever we do, we do together," Nick said. "And we're definitely not risking our lives to get a skull. Sorry Grandma."

Roberta nodded, trying not be angry at them. They were right, of course. Change the subject, Roberta thought. She asked the children about the food for Anthor and laughed out loud when she heard that he had already helped himself to everything they had prepared in the morning to attract him.

"Catching elves is no different from catching fairies. If you blink, you miss them," Roberta told them. "If you want to give it another try, you'll have to go up there and stay up there until he comes back and frankly I think that won't be long. I would guess that, by now, good old Anthor is sure to be hungry again."

When Andrew had said goodnight and all were in their beds, they waited a few minutes before assembling in the kitchen again. Roberta had given both Andrew and Lily a generous cup of Roberta Kibble's Famous Sleeping Potion and now she sat at the kitchen table and Corisander sat on top of it, watching them putting on their shoes.

"Does Corisander know what we're saying?" Ellie asked, looking at the cat.

"I expect he does," Roberta said and lightly poked Corisander. "And sometimes, when I listen closely, I think that he can speak to us, too."

"Meow," Corisander said.

"There you have it," Roberta said, smiling. "Good luck out there."

"You should come, too," Nick said.

Roberta waved her hand as if to swat a fly. She told them that she was too tired when in fact she was too weak. Besides, she didn't expect the elves to ever want to speak to her again. Too much blood on her hands, too many lives on her conscience. Ellie gave her grandmother a quick hug and the boys smiled and waved at her as they stepped out into the night. Good children. Young Archers. Roberta's chest heaved with pride.

Back in the tree where they had hung all the foods in the morning, the children found themselves in a darkness too profound to hang up anything. Nick set the bag down and sat in the place he had occupied before.

"There's no point," Nick said.

"Yeah, we should try again tomorrow," Milo agreed.

"Let's stay anyway," Ellie said and took out the flute. In the safety of the tree she began playing a melancholy Irish tune and the melody drifted deep into the forest. In the warm summer night, the boys leaned their heads against the center of the tree and closed their eyes. The peace of the moment seemed to encircle them.

After a while Nick noticed a new richness to Ellie's melody.

"That's beautiful," Nick said without opening his eyes.

"It's not me," Ellie said in between breaths, then continued playing.

Both Nick and Milo opened their eyes and looked around. As they listened to the music, they realized that another flute was playing, accompanying Ellie's melody, expanding on it, dancing with it in perfect harmony. When Ellie ended her melody, the flute out in the darkness continued for another while, then trailed off into silence.

"Somebody likes your music," Nick said.

"Let's hope it's an elf and not a redcap," Milo added.

Ellie played another melody, then another, trying to entice the unseen player in the forest to join her in music once more. Eventually she shrugged and stopped.

"All of this," Nick began, "All of this will be over soon."

"What do you mean?" Milo asked.

"We'll go back to New York," Ellie said and Nick nodded.

"I'm not," Milo proclaimed.

"When you're fourteen you don't get to choose," Nick replied.

"Shut up," Milo hissed.

"Don't be stupid, there's no –"

"No I mean shut up," Milo urged once more. When they saw Milo staring into the darkness, they followed suit.

"What is it?" Ellie whispered.

"Oh, it's just me," a voice said from above. Their hearts skipped a few beats. They looked up and saw Anthor, smiling at them.

He jumped down, grabbed a chocolate bar from their bag and sat down in their midst.

"Thank you, kind Archers. Today is the best day of my life," Anthor said, unwrapped the chocolate bar and stuffed it whole into his mouth.

"A breakfast like none before and now this," he managed to say while vigorously chewing.

"Did you play the flute, Anthor?" Ellie asked.

"I sing well enough but the instruments have never been my friends," Anthor said as he ripped open a bag of chips. "He's good, isn't he?"

"Who?" Milo asked.

"Oh," Anthor said, his mouth full again. He looked

around and seemed to realize something. "I'm sorry, I thought he was here. He's a bit shy. Desh! Come say hello! Meet the Archers!"

"Desh?" Ellie asked quietly.

"Garondesh, the Bard. He's also our cook. There is so much music in him, sometimes I think he's made of it." Anthor looked around again. "Desh! Come on now!"

After what seemed like a long time, where the only sound was Anthor chewing through the next chocolate bar, another elf appeared. He swung down and sat just a bit apart from the Archers. He looked young and seemed like the physical opposite of Anthor. This elf was very thin and his high cheekbones and pointed noise made him look even more slender. This elf, there was no other way of putting it, was beautiful.

"Desh, these are the Archers," Anthor introduced, pointing to each one of us. "This is Nick, Milo, and that's Ellie – you two have already met, musically speaking."

"Hello," Garondesh said, giving them a nod and a shy smile.

"It's very nice to meet you," Ellie offered. "You play beautifully."

"As do you," Garondesh replied.

"Can I ask you something?" Nick looked at both elves. Garondesh just looked back, Anthor smiled and nodded as he continued eating. "If there was a way to destroy the dome … would you want that?"

"We would be free to go wherever we would want to go," Anthor said.

"We would grow old and die," Garondesh mentioned matter-of-factly.

"Life without the dome? Absolutely. Yes," Anthor proclaimed.

"My answer would also be yes," Garondesh added. "Why do you ask?"

"There may be a way to break the spell," Nick replied.

"Good luck," Anthor uttered. He had discovered a bag of honey-roasted nuts and was now gobbling one after the other. "O'Rein thinks that only Andill himself can destroy what he created. And he's turned himself to stone, so that's that."

"You know about the Rollright Stones," Milo realized.

"Yes, we do know the tale," Garondesh replied. "We know many things. Stories travel, as do melodies," he said with a smile directed at Ellie.

He raised his flute and encouraged her to play again. Garondesh began and Ellie followed and soon the two flutes gently wrapped intertwining melodies around them all. Then, suddenly, Milo leaned forward and motioned for them to be quiet.

Milo looked deadly serious, staring straight down to the ground. In the darkness he saw nothing down there. But when Garondesh and Ellie stopped playing, they all heard a raspy bit of humming coming from down below.

"Don't concern yourself, it's Stope," Garondesh explained.

"He's a fan," Anthor said. "When Desh plays, Stope often shows up to listen. He loves music and I don't think there's a lot of that happening in the tunnels."

"Stope's a redcap?" Nick asked, alarmed.

"He is," Anthor replied.

"You're sure we're safe up here?" Nick asked.

Anthor nodded, pulled the half-empty shopping bag close and searched for his next course. Ellie picked up the melody once more and this time Garondesh followed. Milo leaned back and so did Nick. They shrugged and smiled at each other.

At the house, Roberta leaned on her bedroom window in the dark. She couldn't see the anything, not the children, not the elves. But the music reached her and made her cry.

She didn't wipe her tears as they freely flowed down her cheeks, some splashing onto the window sill, some falling straight into the flowerbed below.

Roberta swallowed hard, breathing in the warmth of the night and the scent of the forest.

In crying, the music made her smile and she realized that she was far from ready to die.

CHAPTER THIRTY-THREE

HOLE IN THE FENCE

It had all begun so well. Roberta felt the way she had not felt in a while. No pain in her legs, no weakness in her back and the smiles came easy. Lily sat at the kitchen table. Corisander snored lightly, stretched out on the window sill that was already warm in the glow of the morning sun.

Andrew had convinced the children to come along to the pool in Witney – just as he often dragged them along in New York. And so, Roberta was alone with Lily and thoroughly enjoyed the one-sided conversation. As always, Lily sat in silence. She was examining the flowing vines and flowers Andrew had drawn on her arms with permanent markers.

Roberta set up an elaborate late breakfast outside on the patio, to be enjoyed with the swimmers once they returned in a little while. She poured herself a cup of Roberta Kibble's Famous Bonding Tea and was thrilled to see that Lily drank some as well. Sitting out on the patio, watching the forest, just talking. This is nice, Roberta thought.

"I know what you're thinking," Roberta said. "It's all too dangerous. So you're saying I shouldn't have called? Well I am dying, I really am. A mother has a right to say goodbye to her daughter, hasn't she?"

Lily took another sip of tea. She kept the cup in her

hands as her eyes roamed from the trees to the sky and from the flowers to the tea before her. Roberta watched her for a while before continuing.

"Yes, yes, true, I did want the children to come here. But I wanted to see my Lily, too," she added softly. "I have hoped, I have always hoped, that Wychwood could make you better. What if ... what if the thing you ran away from is the very thing that can bring you back into life, Lily? I have been thinking that ... what has happened to you happened because of the noise. You remember O'Rein telling us the stories of the creatures going mad with the noise, don't you? And I, and you, and the children ... we do carry within us their blood."

Lily drank from her cup and now her eyes seemed focused on Wychwood. Roberta looked from her to the forest.

"How many times have I sat here wondering who was staring at me from behind the fence. Do you think there's someone there now? I don't sense anything. But if you do, that's a good thing. That's a very good thing."

Without looking at her, Lily held her empty cup in Roberta's direction. Perplexed, Roberta hurried to fill the cup again.

"Lily? Lily, can you hear me?" Roberta asked but Lily just took back the cup, held in both her hands and kept her eyes on the forest.

"So what I'm saying is this," Roberta continued. "There are few places as dangerous as Wychwood, that's true, but Wychwood may also be what you need. Just think, what if you go back to America and one day your children become like you? Away somewhere. Lost somewhere. That's not what you want, is it? Of course that's not what you want … I think you should stay here, Lily."

When Roberta heard movement beyond the fence, it was too late.

***

The children and their father returned in high spirits. When they called for Roberta and no reply came, they didn't worry. When they walked around the house and saw the table all set up, they smiled. Andrew was about to enter the house to look for Roberta and Lily in the kitchen … when Ellie saw it.

"There's a hole in the fence!"

While it took Andrew a moment to understand what Ellie had just shouted, the three children already ran. The hole was dwarf-sized and looked as if it had been hacked open from the inside. Ellie stared at her brothers in horror.

"Grandma! Mom!" Nick yelled at the top of his voice.

"I'm going in," Milo said grimly.

He quickly stepped through the hole but was held back by Nick's hand. Milo tried to tear free but Nick held firm.

"Maybe they're not even in there," Ellie said hurriedly.

"They are," Milo said and stared at Nick. "Let go."

"Don't be stupid," Nick hissed as he saw his father approach. "First of all we don't know what happened and second – you can't go in like this."

"What's going on?" Andrew asked. "What's with the fence? You don't think Grandma took Lily into Wychwood, do you?"

"We're wasting time," Milo said urgently. "Let go!" He tore his arm free and vanished in the thick of the forest.

"Milo!" Ellie shouted.

"Where's Milo going? What the heck is going on?" Andrew asked again. Looking at his children, seeing their faces, he knew that something was terribly wrong. His demeanor changed. "Tell me," he demanded.

For a moment, Nick seemed to blankly gaze at his father, then he suddenly ran off into the shed. Confused, Andrew stared after him.

"What the –" Andrew began and turned to his daughter. "Eliza, I want an explanation. You tell me what is going on here. Now."

Ellie stared up at her father as Milo came through the bushes, back first. Arms hooked under her shoulders, he carried an unconscious Roberta through the hole in the fence and laid her down hurriedly next to Andrew. A large bruise glowed brightly on the side of her head.

"My God," Andrew said. He quickly kneeled, checked her pulse as a thousand things rushed through his head. "Ellie call an ambulance," he said, already standing again. "Your Grandma is … I don't know. Tell them that she was probably struck by a branch. Go, Ellie. I'll look for Lily in the woods. Milo, you check around the house."

Andrew was about to turn and step into the forest, when he noticed that Nick was standing right next to him again.

Nick had a pouch in one hand and a mound of bluish powder in the open palm of his other.

"Sorry, Dad," Nick said and blew the powder in his father's face. Instantly, Andrew wobbled and sagged. Milo caught him and put him next to his grandmother.

"Good thinking," Milo said to Nick.

"Suit up," Nick said. Faces set, they rushed into the shed.

Moments later they were back in their jumper suits, armed and ready. For just an instant they looked down at their father and grandmother.

"We can't just leave them here," Ellie said as she brushed a strand of hair from her grandmother's cheek.

"Caps can't come out here. They're safe. Come on!" Milo rumbled at them as he rushed into the forest.

Nick gave Ellie a nod, then they gave chase.

What remained were two adults stretched out in the grass and a calico cat that hurried across the garden to sit between them.

In the forest, Nick and Ellie caught up with Milo when he stood, eyes closed, listening.

The moment Milo stopped to listen, Nick grabbed him again.

"What do you think happened?" Ellie asked.

"Be quiet," Milo replied, then he turned and looked at her and tried to sound strong and confident. "I'll find her. Ellie. I'll sense her. We have time. Remember I told you about Cowley? They'll take her down into the caves, too."

"Which way?" Nick asked.

"Follow me," Milo said and ran. He was furious because,

while he sensed the wildlife of the forest around him, he didn't sense his mother. Hoping against hope, he ran on.

Milo left the safety of the trees and ran through the underbrush, branches and thorns whipping his face as he did. Wychwood felt alive around him and he was reminded, for just an instant, of his dream. As he ran deeper into the forest, it somehow felt as if the trees around him were not standing still but keeping pace. Still no sense of his mother, Milo stopped, breathing heavily, increasingly distressed.

"We should go up," Ellie huffed breathlessly right behind Milo.

"Faster this way," Milo grimly muttered. "And if we run into redcaps … all the better."

"You're nuts, but you're right," Nick agreed. As a tight unit, they ran on, over dead tree trunks, across clearings and creeks. At times they jumped up into a tree, hurried across branches and descended again, always running. Eventually they stopped and Milo, frustrated, punched a tree trunk hard enough for it to crack.

"What is it?" Ellie asked anxiously.

"Wait here," Milo replied. He swung into the highest tree near them. Maybe altitude would give him what he needed. Moments later, both Nick and Ellie stood next to him.

"What?" Nick asked.

"I have nothing," Milo confessed, tears in his eyes. "I don't sense her. I've tried and I've tried but it's like she's not … anywhere!"

"Maybe they took her into the tunnels already," Nick

said, trying to remain calm. "Do you remember where they attacked the farmer? Or Christopher Smith?"

"Sure," Milo said and threw his hands in the air in irritation. "But it's a maze we don't know anything about – and there are six warrior dwarves like Caark … there's no way we can beat them."

"We need the elves," Ellie said.

"They don't go into the tunnels," Milo said.

"Shendak," Nick shouted suddenly at the top of his voice. "We need your help!"

"Culanxan!" Milo joined in. "Anthor! They have our mother!"

"Garondesh!" Ellie yelled. "O'Rein! Please!"

They called and called and received nothing in return, not from the trees, not from the wind, not from the birds. An unnatural silence followed their calls.

"Then we go in alone," Nick said grimly. Both Milo and Ellie looked at him, straightened their backs and nodded. "Where's the nearest hatch?"

CHAPTER THIRTY-FOUR

IN THE REALM
OF THE REDCAPS

Less than five minutes later Nick, Milo and Ellie stood just a few paces from the place where the redcaps had brought farmer Cowley underground. The hatch was invisible but Milo was certain that they were in the right place.

"It's right there," Milo said.

They checked in every direction, as if expecting redcaps to jump out at them from behind every bush and tree, then hurried to the hatch. Milo pushed aside leaves and twigs and there it was. Nick reached for the handle.

"You ready?" he asked.

"No," Ellie said tensely. "But Mom's down there."

Nick was about to pull on the hatch, when a booming voice stopped him.

"Wait."

They whirled around and saw Shendak descend from a nearby tree. Behind him, one after the other, the rest of the elves followed. There was Culanxan, approaching stoically.

There was Anthor, looking far more serene than usual. And there were O'Rein and Garondesh, both of them nodding as they came to a stop next to Shendak.

"We've been calling," Nick said evenly.

"We heard," Shendak replied. "Your mother is not in the forest, Archers."

"She is," Milo shot back.

"No," O'Rein said calmly. "We would have sensed her."

"We found Grandma unconscious in the forest," Ellie said.

"And the fence torn open from the inside," Nick added.

"Mom's in the forest," Milo insisted. "And we're wasting time."

Shendak gave Anthor a questioning look.

"She's not. She can't be. I would know, I was South post until just now," Anthor replied. "I would have noticed," he added defensively.

"Did you sense Roberta?" Culanxan evenly asked.

"No, but –" Anthor started.

"Then you might be wrong about Lily, too," Culanxan said.

"I wasn't sleeping on post," Anthor said heatedly. "I know it's happened once or twice but that was four hundred years ago. I did not sleep!"

For a moment, everyone's eyes were on Shendak.

"We're going in," he said.

Nick grabbed hold of the handle and pulled on the hatch with all his might. It didn't move an inch. Anthor pulled him aside.

"Allow me," he said.

"What about the element of surprise?" O'Rein asked.

"I want them to know that we are coming," Shendak said

and gave Anthor a nod.

From where he stood, Anthor jumped high into the air. He seemed to soar for a moment and then, at the highest point, he straightened his legs and crossed his arms across his chest. Like a massive tree trunk, he slammed through the hatch with a crash and was gone. The sound of the crash reverberated down in the tunnel.

"Clear," Anthor's voice came from the darkness below.

"Archers," O'Rein said as they all checked their weapons one last time. "Elves have never ventured into the realm of the caps because they have the advantage down there. Remember, while we don't wish to kill them – they will not hesitate."

"Together," Shendak said. For a moment, his hand rested on Milo's shoulder. Then he jumped into the hole, followed instantly by the other elves. Ellie swallowed hard but was first to follow the elves. Nick and Milo nodded each other.

"We're going to save Mom," Nick said.

"We're going to save Mom," Milo repeated.

Ropes hooked into the tree above, they sailed down into the tunnel. For a moment, they saw absolutely nothing. Milo gave a start when he heard Shendak's voice next to him.

"When you were down here last, which way did they take their captive?"

Milo stared intently and quickly his eyes adjusted to the light below.

"That way," he said and pointed.

"Cul, point. Anthor, rear," Shendak ordered. His gaze went from elf to elf and came to rest on the children. "They know that we're coming. They may be angry, but they're also confused by our presence. Stay behind us. Don't think, trust your instincts as your grandmother has taught you."

"Ready?" Culanxan asked.

"Ready," Milo replied.

A smile played around Culanxan's mouth, then he screamed at the top of his lungs and charged forward. The other elves followed suit and so did the Archers. Like a horizontal avalanche of fury, they rolled through the tunnels and their screams charged ahead of them. In running Milo saw the skull he had used to knock Urk unconscious.

"That's as far as I came!"

"No matter, I can smell them!" Culanxan called back without slowing down. As the group of rescuers charged around the next bend, they almost slammed into a massive door. It was locked and despite Anthor's hammering, it didn't move.

"I'll open it," O'Rein said with calm confidence.

"No time," Shendak said and motioned to Anthor. Anthor nodded and ran against the door from a good distance. Loose rocks rained down on them, the walls cracked in places – but the door didn't break. After the third attempt, Anthor shook his head and gave up.

"When you're done, maybe I can give it a try," O'Rein suggested. He took a pouch and rolled it out. It looked remarkably like a set of lock picks.

"You shouldn't have come down here," a familiar voice said loudly from behind the door. "Here, we rule. Here, you cannot escape into the trees."

"You're right, Urk. We made a mistake coming down here. Please open the door so that we may apologize," Anthor said. The others all readied their bows and arrows, swords and knives. The children, in the midst of the elves, pulled out their knives and hatchets, too.

"Do you think I'm stupid?" Urk asked through the door.

"In your case, stupid doesn't even come close," Anthor said with a grin. Instantly something crashed against the other side of the door and a howl followed. "Did you hurt your head?" Anthor asked gleefully.

"Anthor," Urk's fuming voice called, "when the others are here I will personally take your head."

"So I guess you're alone then," O'Rein said pleasantly. "Hold on, Urk, we'll be with you in a minute."

"What do you mean?" Urk called back, sounding worried. O'Rein used a variety of tools, sending turning, twisting and scraping sounds to the other side. "What are you doing?" Urk shouted, fear mixed into his anger.

"Just coming to see you," O'Rein said.

"O'Rein likes opening locks," Garondesh said to Ellie.

"In the old days," Anthor explained, "travelers would sometimes leave their lives as well as their chests of valuables behind. It's become somewhat of a pastime for O'Rein."

"Caark and Taar are here," Urk called but he sounded

too scared for it to be true.

"The more the merrier!" Anthor called back. O'Rein twisted another lock pick and, with loud clicks, several locks in the door snapped open. O'Rein got to his feet and smiled as Anthor grabbed the door and swung it open. The elves readied their bows and arrows.

With the door wide open, they saw another long tunnel – and Urk running as fast as his short legs carried him. Culanxan's arrow flew and hit Urk in the left thigh.

The dwarf yelled, cursed and disappeared, limping, at the far end.

"Move!" Shendak yelled and with a roar, the charge continued.

CHAPTER THIRTY-FIVE

THE BATTLE
IN THE TROPHY HALL

They entered together, five elves and three Archers, weapons at the ready.

Milo looked to Nick and Ellie and saw that they were just as surprised. The tunnel had taken them further and further down and when they entered, they understood why. What they looked at wasn't an underground cave but a vast hall that, at some point in time, had no doubt been the pride of the redcaps.

The hall was carved into the rock far below Wychwood with great skill. There were pillars and alcoves, large tables and benches all seemingly carved out of the one single rock formation. But what once had been as impressive as a palace of nobility was now no more than the dwarves' living quarters.

In the instant they rushed into the hall, they took in the bunks in the corners, the rock chipped and broken, and refuse everywhere.

Ellie shuddered at the pile of bones in one corner and she saw that that the elves were no less taken aback than they were. Some of the kills were still fresh, as if they had only just been brought down.

The one thing that made them doubt their courage more than anything else were the trophies. In the countless alcoves along the walls were the massive heads of giants, the wide skulls of dragons, the familiar shapes of humans and many smaller and oddly shaped ones as well.

"I don't see Mom," Nick told Shendak.

"Silence," Shendak commanded.

He looked at the elves, at the Archers, leaving no doubt that he would take the lead. As the children anxiously looked around for their mother, they all remembered Chester Archer. One of the many skulls in this room had to be the one their grandmother so desperately wanted returned to the surface.

At the far end of the hall, by the imposing raised throne, stood the six redcaps. It seemed that they had all only just assembled. They were cursing and scrambling to arm themselves. Their leader, a gray-maned redcap named Tonk, sat on the throne. To his left was Caark, to his right Taar. Urk was next to them, sweating and swearing as he pulled Culanxan's arrow from his leg. He spit at it and tossed it aside, almost hitting the other two dwarves, one was the music loving redcap they called Stope, the other was one-eyed Gerg.

"You have come to die, Shendak," Tonk pointed out calmly from the throne.

"We have not even come to fight," Shendak replied. "If you return the woman, we will leave peacefully."

Tonk leaned over to Taar and the others weighed in on a heated conversation the children couldn't hear. Then he addressed Shendak once more.

"She is ours, head and blood," Tonk claimed with a savage grin.

"Where is our mother?!" Milo yelled and Nick took aim at Tonk, knife in hand.

"If you win, you can have her," Tonk called gleefully.

O'Rein quickly stepped in front of the Archers.

"They don't have her," he whispered.

"What do you mean?" Nick asked, lowering his knife.

"Our ears pick up on their whispers as easily as if they were screaming," Garondesh explained. "Tonk just asked the others and neither one of them knows anything about a woman in the forest."

"But that's impossible," Ellie said.

"That's the one, Tonk," Caark grunted, aiming his pike straight at Milo. "That one is mine. That head is my head."

In one swift motion, Tonk's fist connected with Caark's temple and the powerful redcap almost fell. Furious, he glared back at Tonk.

"You decide nothing, Caark. Battle well and I may let you have his head."

Tonk slowly rose and was handed a pike by Taar. As he walked down the steps from the throne, the others assembled next to him. The elves' arrows were all aimed at Tonk who didn't seem worried in the slightest.

"If we stay, there will be death," O'Rein whispered.

Shendak barely nodded.

"Retreat," he said.

"Oh, you are not leaving," Tonk called. "Your presence

has soiled our halls and your blood will wash it clean." He slammed his pike down on a rock in the ground. A mechanism instantly activated and collapsed the tunnel behind the elves.

"Attack!" Tonk yelled and the battle began.

Both the elves and the dwarves moved with incredible speed and Nick, Ellie and Milo had their hands full just trying to stay alive.

When Tonk launched the attack, the elves' arrows were loosed. But Tonk, with improbable elegance, slipped aside as the arrows smashed uselessly into the steps of the throne. Every long-distance attack was foiled by the dwarves with the use of their pikes to smash arrows aside.

The same on the other side. The one named Gerg used a crossbow to kill Shendak but the leader of the elves was far too fast. In moving, he also pulled Ellie and O'Rein aside who would have been hit by the arrow of the crossbow.

With the dwarves charging and the avenue of retreat blocked, the elves and Archers alike had no other way but to advance as well. Shendak pointed toward another tunnel on the opposite side of the hall – the only way to get there was through a pack of lethal redcaps.

"That way!"

Culanxan was locked in combat with Taar. Garondesh brandished two curved swords and fought against the mud-caked Stope. O'Rein took on Gerg and Anthor slammed into Urk. In the midst of it all Shendak and Tonk clashed.

The clamor of metal echoing off the walls, the dust rising in the air and the intensity of not just watching these warriors, but of being in the thick of it was almost too much for the Archers.

How were they supposed to be a match for warriors who had battled for thousands of years? They had no time to be afraid, retreat or avoid. As best they could they launched their own attacks, parried, ducked, rolled … and through it all Caark came closer and closer to Milo.

"Come now, little Archer – time to die!" he shouted.

Nick fought off a stab by Urk and tried to join Milo. More than once they saved each other's lives.

As Nick ducked away once more it was only thanks to Ellie that Gerg's pike didn't pierce through him. As the battle raged on, the children noticed how Shendak and the others managed to gradually move the battle to the tunnel in the back.

In the heat of the fight, Milo activated the rage instinctively. All of a sudden he was as fast, and faster, then those around him. He helped O'Rein wipe Urk off his feet, broke Stope's pike in half … and didn't see Caark coming at him from behind.

At the last second Nick's hatchet came flying and hit Caark squarely between the eyes with the blunt side. He howled in pain, but charged once more. Stumbling backwards, Milo seemed lost as Caark came at him. To his surprise, he fell.

Ellie had picked up a dropped pike and wedged it between his running legs. Caark crashed head first into a

243

pillar where he rolled on the floor, dazed.

When Milo looked up, he was startled to see an alcove near the throne, engraved with arrows all around it. In the alcove, a single human skull. Without thinking, Milo ran and grabbed it.

"Now!" Shendak shouted at the children and looked to Culanxan. Culanxan nodded. O'Rein, Garondesh, Anthor and the Archers ran into the tunnel.

Looking back, they saw that Gerg was firing off another arrow from his crossbow.

"Watch out, Nick!" Milo yelled. Nick looked up, saw the arrow coming at him, unable to move, too late to move. Shendak pushed Nick aside, the arrow instead burying itself in Shendak's shoulder. He grit his teeth.

"Archers, go. Go now, we will hold them. Find your mother!"

Anthor grabbed them by their suits and yanked them into the tunnel. With his bulk he kept pushing them forward as they tried to see what was happening behind them. The last thing they saw, just before Anthor pushed them around a bend in the tunnel, was Shendak and Culanxan standing at the end of the tunnel, blocking it against the onslaught of the redcaps.

Moments later Anthor effortlessly threw Milo up onto the forest floor. They had discovered a vertical shaft and Anthor, O'Rein and Garondesh had pushed up the Archers in a hurry. Garondesh covered the rear until they were all up in the light of day again.

"We have to go back," Milo said and tried to push past

Anthor, but the big elf stood firm and shook his head.

"Is that …?" Nick said, pointing at the skull in Milo's hand.

"Yeah, Chester," Milo replied.

O'Rein climbed from the tunnel, followed by Garondesh. Anthor remained at the open hatch and listened. There was only silence.

O'Rein shook his head.

Garondesh wiped away a tear and Ellie buried her face in Nick's chest. Then, from far below, they heard a distant murmur that soon grew into shouts and the clanging of metal. Hope rising, they looked at the hatch and were stunned when suddenly Shendak and Culanxan rushed up and out of the tunnel.

Culanxan slammed the hatch shut and stood on it. Both he and Shendak had several arrows protruding from their arms, shoulders, legs and chest. They were also covered with cuts across their faces and their outfits looked shredded … and they smiled.

"Most fun I have had in a thousand years," Shendak said as he pulled the arrows from his body. Culanxan remained on the hatch as someone was pounding against it from underneath.

"You've had your chance," Culanxan called down. He also removed the arrows, barely wincing, then he and Shendak embraced and laughed out loud.

"I will kill you!" Tonk's voice, mad with fury, came from below. "I will kill you and I will kill those children and I will kill their mother. Your heads will be mine!" Tonk continued cursing and muttering as he climbed down the shaft.

The smiling elves embraced, patted each other on shoulders and backs, Anthor and Culanxan even chest bumped. The Archers glanced at each other, feeling more than a little left out and yet, caught in the moment, also smiling. Suddenly, O'Rein and Anthor stepped to them and hugged them as well. Then all the elves encircled them. The children glowed.

O'Rein took a small wooden box from one of his pockets and took a handful of brown paste from it. This paste he rubbed onto the wounds of Shendak and Culanxan whenever he got them to hold still for a moment. They didn't seem to mind their wounds. As the children found out later, the elves had a higher threshold for pain and their bodies healed more quickly. As fast as the joy had spread, it was ended by Shendak.

"We still have to find your mother," he said to Nick, Milo and Ellie.

"But if the redcaps don't have here, she's safe, right?" Ellie asked.

"Yes, likely," O'Rein said, smiling at her. "But she could be anywhere and Tonk will send them all out to look for her. There are tunnels under all of Wychwood and they could come up in any part of Wychwood at any time."

Shendak readied his rope and they all did the same … except for Nick. He had noticed movement in the bushes and suddenly saw Taar standing there, his pike aimed and ready to be hurled at Shendak's back.

Nick acted on instinct. In a single flow, he pulled and threw the knife. Shendak merely glimpsed the knife – it flew fast and hard and buried itself to the hilt in Taar's forehead. For a moment, Taar still stood. He threw the pike, but neither strength nor aim were with him anymore. Shendak pulled his sword and effortlessly deflected the pike. As it clattered against a tree trunk, Taar fell and lay dead.

For an instant, no one moved. Then Anthor pulled the knife from Taar's skull, wiped it clean on the ground and handed it back to its owner. Nick sheathed it without looking away from Taar. Milo stepped next to his brother on one side, Ellie on the other.

"I killed him," Nick murmured flatly.

"This won't exactly improve Tonk's mood," Anthor said with a grin. His grin disappeared when he saw O'Rein shaking his head.

"You had no choice," Milo told Nick and Ellie grabbed her big brother's arm as if to steady him. He gave her a paper-thin smile.

"I can't ... breathe." Nick looked at them blankly and going pale.

Shendak grabbed him by the shoulders and shook him. He looked deep into Nick's eyes.

"This is the second time an Archer has saved my life," he said. "Robert the Archer was the first. I thank you."

"I killed him," Nick said again, looking at Shendak with wide open eyes.

"Your brother is wrong when he said you had no

choice," Shendak explained. "You did. I am glad you chose as you did – but you now need to learn to live with it. You have killed and Taar's face will remain with you through time."

Nick took a deep breath, then nodded. During this exchange the other elves had been on high alert, guarding every direction.

"What do we do – with him?" Nick asked.

"Where he is, is where he should be," O'Rein said. "The forest will feast."

They ascended into the trees and the elves stopped ever so often to let their senses roam in search of the children's mother. Milo sensed nothing but animals and saw, from the frowns on the faces of the elves, that they perceived no more than he did.

They were just about to push on, when something akin an earthquake shook the ground and the trees and rippled across all of the forest.

"What was that?" Nick asked.

"I don't know," Shendak said.

"It was a call," O'Rein said. "A tremor of the flow."

"How can that be?" Culanxan asked.

"It can't," Shendak said grimly, then pointed east. "It came from Rutland Plain."

Without another word he swung off, followed instantly by elves and Archers.

CHAPTER THIRTY-SIX

THE OLD KING

They landed under the cover of the forest, with just one thick row of bushes separating them from the plain.

"We're close to Wort's Well, right?" Milo whispered.

O'Rein nodded, his finger to his lips. The elves were concentrated on the forest around them. They had to expect redcaps coming at them at any given moment. Not only had they invaded their trophy hall, they had also killed one of them. Tonk would not let it stand and Tonk could not, for fear of showing weakness.

Shendak gave each of them a glance, adjusted a knife on Nick's suit, gave Ellie and Milo a quick smile, then nodded at all of them. He pushed through the bushes, leading the way onto Rutland Plain. When the Archers stood on the plain, they were as stunned as the elves at the sight before them.

There, in the middle of the clearing, sat Ashford Bromley, together with Lily Archer. To his left sat Jim Jam, still as a statue. Bromley and Lily seemed to be completely at ease inside a circle of dozens of deer, boars, badgers, foxes and other forest creatures. It appeared as if Ashford Bromley was holding court. While Lily looked into the trees, Bromley was staring straight at the new arrivals.

"Mom!" Ellie called and tried to rush forward.

Anthor held her back and shook his head at Nick and Milo.

"That is not Ashford Bromley," O'Rein whispered.

As the animals rose, many more were revealed, smaller ones, squirrels and weasels, marten and mice. Birds large and small flew across the clearing, woodpeckers and blackbirds, buzzards and jays. They landed in the trees from where they watched intently. The eyes of all of Wychwood seemed to be on the elves … and especially on the Archers.

Bromley took hold of his staff and got to his feet.

"Ashford," Shendak called, "we are glad to see that you have found Lily."

Bromley, in unusual stillness, said nothing. He breathed, deeply. Letting his gaze roam across the clearing, he smiled.

"Who are you?" O'Rein asked.

"I am the Old King. I am all," Ashford replied in a rumbling voice that wasn't his.

O'Rein shot Shendak and the others a glance and shrugged.

"We are honored by your presence," O'Rein said, playing along. "Welcome to our forest."

"My forest!" The Old King boomed and his voice shook the trees. Birds scattered and the animals in the plain shivered. When calm had returned, the Old King continued, serenely now. "I have slept but now I am awake. What you see within the dome and without, is mine."

"Why have you called this woman to you?" O'Rein asked, indicating Lily.

"She is the mother of freedom. She has brought me the younglings," the Old King replied and looked at Nick, Milo and Ellie. "Come to me."

As the Old King lifted his hand and pointed at the children, an energy rose in the plain and the children felt themselves being pulled.

"Protect the children," Shendak said and instantly, Culanxan, Anthor and Garondesh stepped in front of them.

"What's going on?" Anthor asked anxiously. "Who's the Old King?"

"I don't know," O'Rein said. "Be prepared."

"Come to me!" the Old King shouted and again his voice sent a ripple through Wychwood.

"We have to get Mom," Nick said.

"We have to be cautious," Culanxan replied evenly. "Be patient. Be calm. And stop pushing," he added as he felt Nick pushing against his back.

To their surprise the Archers realized that they seemed to have no control over their bodies. The pull forced them toward the Old King and only the elves were standing in their way. Nick suddenly imagined that it must have been this force that had brought mother and grandmother into Wychwood.

"Hold them, tight," Shendak ordered.

Culanxan, Anthor and Garondesh wrapped their arms around the Archers and found themselves straining to keep in place. Even when the elves lifted them off the ground, the force of the Old King's pull did not lessen.

"Come to me!" the Old King said for the third time.

"What's happening with us!?" Ellie said, looking at Nick and Milo, then at her own arms.

Struggling in the arms of the elves, the bodies of the Archers seemed to lose form.

"O'Rein, something's happening – help!" Milo shouted.

O'Rein and Shendak helplessly watched as the bodies of the Archers began to pulse with energy, began to flow with the air. An instant passed and then they flowed through the arms of the elves and began walking toward the Old King.

"There's nothing I can do!" Nick shouted.

The elves reached for the children again and again but their hands went through them as if they were nothing but vapor.

"My goodness," O'Rein said to Shendak, "they're flowen!"

As the Archers approached the center of the plain, the animals began to move. With an ever-increasing speed, they raced each other in a circle around the Old King and Lily Archer. The circle became a wall of hoofs and horns, antlers and tusks, teeth and beaks.

The elves, unwilling to give up, again reached for the children but without success. As they approached the circle of the animals, the children passed through it without resistance.

Culanxan charged and leaped high to vault past the

animals. As he did, he was hit by a dozen large owls and fell to the ground with owls still clawing and pecking at his face. He whirled around, ran forward once more, only to be rammed by Jim Jam. Just as he tried, so did the others … and all failed. Powerless, they stood and watched as the children came to a halt in the middle of the circle before the Old King.

Ellie rushed to her mother and, realizing that she was solid form again, embraced her fiercely.

"Mom's okay. Mom's okay," she kept repeating.

On the other side of the plain the redcaps appeared. Anger mixed with confusion when Tonk saw what was happening in the middle. Then he saw the woman.

"There she is! Bring her to me, head and blood!"

A massive boar grunted, lowered its head and attacked Caark who had been first to step out into the clearing. Caark put his pike aside and imitated the boar. Head down, he charged. When the heads of boar and redcap connected, both fell to the side, momentarily dazed. But Caark was first to rise – he kicked the boar and continued toward the center. In the end, however, the redcaps were as powerless as the elves and finally came to a standstill, infuriated and exhausted, on opposite sides of the animal circle.

"You have come. Now free me," the Old King said and reached for Milo. The grip around Milo's wrist was powerful and the heat emanating from his hand felt like ten thousand rages. Milo screamed. Nick and Ellie rushed to tear their brother away from the old man but as they touched Milo, the surge of energy rushed through them as well. The Archers screamed in excruciating pain and couldn't let go as if glued to the Old King.

The Old King began to glow and a blissful smile spread across his face. Wychwood was shaking. Trees were uprooted and crashed to the ground, elves and dwarves were thrown off their feet and, panicked, the animals fled in all directions.

The livid Tonk jumped to his feet just to be felled again. Shendak, keeping his eyes on the redcaps, fared no better. As the ground kept shaking, they were helpless, advancing inches just to be thrown back again.

The Old King stopped smiling as the increasing surge of energy coursed through the earth, through the Archers and into him.

"Enough," he croaked but couldn't let go of Milo. Ashford Bromley's body lost shape, expanded, the spirit now a large pulsing swirl of color.

Somewhere beyond the pain Milo thought that he was looking at the flow itself. That it was what the world must have looked like in the beginning.

It was mesmerizingly beautiful.

"Too much!" the Old King screamed in agony.

Then the colors exploded out of Ashford Bromley, through the Archers, through the elves and redcaps and through all of Wychwood.

The Old King's scream reverberated for another moment and then silence returned.

The Archers and their mother lay unconscious and the thin body of Ashford Bromley was curled up next to them.

For a moment, nothing moved.

When Tonk got to his feet, kicking the others and pointing at Lily Archer, Shendak realized that nothing had changed between them.

The elves ran forward.

Each one of them shouldered a human and rushed them to the safety of the trees.

CHAPTER THIRTY-SEVEN

FAMILY MATTERS

Corisander had been in the barn at Cowley's farm. He had enjoyed watching owls and there currently was a brood of seven fuzzy chicks in the rafters of Cowley's barn. Because of that, Corisander had missed the cutting of the fence by the possessed Bromley, the abduction of Lily – and the failed rescue attempt by Roberta. He only rushed back to the house of the Archers when Wychwood shook and shivered with the forces of the flow.

Corisander found Roberta and Andrew, unconscious. He sensed into her and knew that Roberta would be fine. The headache and bruise would be dealt with swiftly by Roberta's famous teas and balms. Standing on Andrew's chest, Corisander could make out traces of memory-erasing powder on the man's face. There was nothing for Corisander to do but to sit and wait. Something was happening in the forest, something that had not happened since the creation of the dome.

When finally there was movement on the other side of the fence, Corisander jumped to the hole. He didn't know whether to be relieved or concerned when he saw all of the elves swinging into view and landing up in the tree, the children, Lily and Bromley over their shoulders. They placed them gently onto comfortable branches, then

O'Rein began attending them one by one. Corisander could smell the ointments and had no doubt that the humans were receiving the best of care up there.

Nick was the first to wake. Dazed, he looked around. He saw Garondesh dabbing Ellie's face with a cloth. Milo was coming to and O'Rein just finished applying a balm to a scar across Milo's nose. Then Nick saw his mother and Bromley, both of them unconscious. He wanted to rush up but Culanxan pushed him back, gently but firmly.

"Everyone is fine," Culanxan explained.

"Bromley. He's …?" Nick began.

"Just good old Ashford again," Anthor offered.

"What happened?" Milo asked, frowning, looking around and only after a moment realizing where they were.

"Your questions are our questions, Milo," O'Rein replied as he sat down next to Bromley to check for injuries. "I can only tell you that an ancient spirit spoke through him."

"I thought they were all gone," Ellie mentioned.

"As did we," Shendak said.

"Grandma told us about Andill and Ardunn," Nick wondered. "Maybe that's who the Old King was."

"Ardunn died when he tried to free us," O'Rein replied. "We were there when the spell that was meant to destroy the dome destroyed him instead."

"We may never know the name of the spirit," Garondesh suggested. "He is gone. And we are here. Safe," he added with a smile.

"Why did he want us?" Milo asked.

"In you, he saw the power he needed to free himself,"

O'Rein replied. "You saw it for yourself. When you transformed, that was the flow in you."

"That was real?" Ellie asked.

"Oh yes," Garondesh replied.

"That wasn't us, that was the spirit," Nick said.

"The spirit just brought it out in you," O'Rein explained. "You have always had the flow within you. And who knows, maybe, over time, you will learn to master it."

As Corisander lay in the grass below, he wondered. He listened to the conversations up in the tree and the more he heard, the more he worried. It appeared that the spirit had vanished, not a trace of him left, destroyed by the children's energy he had tried to possess. It was true enough, Corisander sensed nothing now. No reverberations … and no pull. There was only a forest named Wychwood.

"It is time," Shendak said.

Garondesh lightly bowed, pulled out his flute and handed it to Ellie.

"I hope we may play again." He smiled and Ellie blushed as she accepted the gift.

"I'm so hungry I could eat a tree," Anthor proclaimed as he rose. "A chocolate-coated tree, of course." He slapped Garondesh on the back and together they jumped off into the trees. Culanxan lifted the still unconscious Bromley onto his shoulder and shook the hands of the Archers in turn, slowly, reverently. To the children it felt as if they were being knighted. With the hint of a smile on his lips, Culanxan nodded and jumped off.

"Robert the Archer would be proud," O'Rein suggested. He had put away potions and ointments and now stood before the Archers. "As am I." He bowed and vanished in the forest.

Only Shendak remained. For once, he seemed ill at ease as he looked down into the garden of the Archer house. Roberta was waking up, shaking her head and groaning. Next to her, the children's father stirred.

"I saw that you recovered Chester's head," Shendak said without looking at Milo. His eyes remained on Roberta. "Your grandmother will be pleased. You should go now, before your father sees you."

Shendak lowered Lily to the garden side of the fence. Her eyes were open now and she looked around in confusion. Corisander rose and leaned against her leg, purring. Frowning, she bent down and began stroking the cat.

Roberta hurried to Lily and embraced her. Behind her, Andrew approached as well, still half asleep. He looked up into the tree just before Shendak disappeared.

"Be safe," Shendak said with a smile and was gone.

"What was ... what's going on?" Andrew asked.

"Where to begin," Lily replied.

Corisander was as amazed as the rest of them. The children forgot about their suits and jumped out of the tree. Andrew stared from them back to Lily and a smile began spreading across Roberta's face.

"Lily," Andrew whispered in a mere hush. "Did you just speak?"

Lily looked at him, smiled and kissed him.

"Yes," she said.

"Yes!" Andrew shouted, lifted her up and jumped around and around, drunk with joy. When he finally let her down, Lily looked at her mother and her children.

"I think it's time for you to tell us a tale of Wychwood."

What followed was an evening of revelations and revelry. Roberta and the children first told Andrew about the world beyond the fence, then brought him down into the armory and through it all, as he marveled at everything he had never considered possible, they explained the flow and fairy creatures and their connection to it.

Corisander was glad to see how well Andrew took it all and knew that tomorrow more explanations would be required. For now he floated on the love for his wife and the remnants of the powder still affecting him. He would sleep well and wake, wondering whether all of this had been a dream. But then his wife would be next to him and she would wake him with a kiss and a smile and a loving word.

They did keep many of the occurrences to themselves. The fights with the redcaps, the abduction by an ancient spirit … and Chester's head, too.

When Andrew and Lily had left the shed, Milo held Roberta back and handed her the skull.

"We got lucky," Milo admitted.

Roberta started at the skull, then at Milo, then at the skull again.

"This is Chester?" she asked with a trembling voice.

"Yes," Milo replied.

"Are you sure?"

"I'm sure," Milo replied and told her about the unique alcove adorned with arrow carvings. Her hands shaking, Roberta gently took the skull from Milo and brought it to the rest of her brother's skeleton. In a whisper, she told him that he would finally be buried ... and then she cried. When she returned to the children, Roberta embraced them one by one and ushered them out of the armory.

The evening was a feast of food and drink and tales and music and through it all one question lingered ... Lily was awake again. In the place she had never wanted to return to. She laughed and sang and danced and when, late at night, they could all barely keep their eyes open, Lily spoke.

"Do you think you could live here, Andrew?"

Her question brought instant silence to the room. Nick, Milo, Ellie and their grandmother held their breath. Andrew looked from them to Lily and smiled.

"I can write anywhere," he offered.

"Could we stay?" Lily asked Roberta.

Roberta sniffled and tears flowed freely as she stepped forward and embraced her daughter. Andrew grinned happily, at them, at his children.

The three of them stood, just slightly apart and watched it all.

"New best day ever," Milo said.

ANDILL

Even with the beginning of the next day, Corisander felt how the flow around the house had begun to change. There had been lies and deception and everyone knew that explanations would need to be given and they knew that those explanations wouldn't be enough for a time to come.

How could Roberta bring them here, well knowing that she would endanger the lives of the children? How could Andrew agree to the trip when Lily had made her wishes unmistakably clear? How could the children lie to their father time and time again?

As they all sat at the kitchen table, enjoying the vast breakfast buffet Roberta had prepared, they all wished that they could go back to the celebrations of the night before. Corisander knew them, he knew them so well.

Roberta did all she could to keep them happy and busy. Even the lavish buffet had been put together mostly to keep everyone's mouths occupied. Conversations could not be avoided, but they most certainly could be delayed for another while.

As soon as the first of them were finished, Roberta spoke up.

"Francis is going to take us to the Rollright Stones – he'll be here in a few minutes so we should all get ready," she said and hurried out of the room.

"She feels guilty," Andrew said.

"She should," Lily replied. She looked at the children and sighed. "I have no idea how any of this will work. I remember what it means to be an Archer."

"We have saved two men's lives," Nick said.

"We're good," Milo said.

"And we'll always be with the elves," Ellie added. "Do you know about the Rollright Stones?" she asked, trying to switch topic.

While Lily remembered the tale of Andill and Ardunn, Andrew knew only the little they had told him the night before. The children took turns retelling what Francis and Roberta had shared with them and it was Ellie who enacted the witch who turned the king and his men to stone.

When she was done, Roberta stood in the door, dressed up and ready to go.

"Nicely told, Ellie," she said. She ushered them out of their chairs and just five minutes later they were all outside in the drive way, waiting for their pickup.

Corisander watched them from the garden. He didn't need to be able to tell the future to know that they really would stay. They would stay by purpose and by necessity. This was the place where Archers belonged … and this was the place that had brought Lily back. Corisander had listened to her telling the others about the past years.

She had disappeared into a world where there had been neither noise nor concern, neither darkness nor pain. To Lily it had always felt like floating in a warm green cloud, as if nature itself had wrapped her up for protection. Now they knew, just as Corisander knew – that their elfish selves would always need the quiet.

This had been Lily's home in the past and it would be her home once again. Corisander felt the weariness in her heart as she wondered how she could ever allow her children to enter Wychwood again. She wasn't like Roberta ... and her heart grew heavier still with the thought of her mother dying.

The Oakham Park estate's green minibus turned into the driveway and stopped before them.

Lord Francis Thornton exited and opened the sliding doors on both sides. Roberta approached him and curtseyed as she always did.

Francis grinned at her.

"Roberta told me about your adventure yesterday," he said exuberantly, shaking the children's hands. "But I'll want to hear it all again, of course – my goodness, the flow! I must tell you, I have never been this hopeful!" he added cheerfully.

"Nice to see you again, Francis," Andrew shook Francis hand – then Francis stopped right in front of Lily.

"Say something. Anything."

"Good morning, Lord Thornton," Lily obliged with a smile.

"Please do call me Francis!" he exclaimed, beaming. "This is a spectacular day, I dare say. What are we waiting for? Shall we?"

Corisander smiled a cat's smile from where he lay. The

lord's excitement was infectious, he saw it spreading to the others instantly as they hopped into the minibus on either side. Francis remained at the sliding door.

"Well, let's go," Roberta said from the passenger seat.

"We're not complete yet," Francis said and looked at the cat. "What do you say, Corisander. Care for a drive?"

Amused, Corisander looked at Francis standing there.

Why not, he thought, slowly rose and meandered to the minibus. He hopped in and sat on Lily's lap. Francis gave him a wink as he slid the door closed.

They left the house behind and drove toward Charlbury. As they drove by the house of Christopher Smith, the children saw the old man working in his yard on one of his monster sculptures. He looked worn, sad and lost.

"I want to tell him," Ellie said. Roberta frowned but Corisander saw acceptance in the eyes of Nick and Milo. Corisander had a feeling that a dexterous man such as Christopher Smith would become a valuable ally. He could already see him in the armory, improving on everything he could get his hands on.

"So …," Francis began. "Everybody knows everything, correct? We can speak openly in our little circle of friends?"

"Meow," Corisander said and everyone laughed.

Instantly Francis jumped into the world of magic and didn't stop until they arrived at the Rollright Stones thirty minutes later.

He told them about Andill and every scrap of research, from the interpretation of ancient scrolls to the hidden meanings of poems and songs of old. It was nothing new to Corisander.

"If the King Stone is indeed Andill, that is," Francis mused, looked back at them for a moment and almost swerved off the road. "Terribly sorry!"

"You've waited a lifetime, Francis," Roberta suggested calmly. "It would be such a shame to die in a traffic accident now, wouldn't it?"

"Indeed," Francis agreed. "I shall keep my eyes on the road."

"And you might also consider slowing down," Roberta added.

"Of course," Francis conceded. "My apologies. All this excitement, the anticipation."

"You think something will happen?" Andrew asked.

"I don't know. But then I don't think there has ever been an instant where three flowen came to the Rollright Stones."

"Flowen?" Andrew asked, confused.

"I thought everybody knew everything," Francis replied.

"You're flowen?" Lily asked, looking at the children in wonder.

"What's a flowen?" Andrew asked again.

"Flowen are shapeshifters, Dad," Ellie explained.

"Wait, you're what?!"

"Flowen! Shapeshifters! It's a good thing," Francis called back to Andrew. "I can assure you. A very good thing, a powerful thing. And there's three of them. Three! Imagine the three of them coming together with Andill!"

It was early afternoon when the green minibus parked on the side of a narrow road.

As they left the vehicle, they were met by a perfect summer day. Blue skies greeted them and a blackbird sang in one of the trees that hid the circle of stones called the King's Men. But they had not come here to meet the king's men, they had come to meet the king and the King Stone stood, imposing, in the open field across the road.

A hush had come over the land and even the blackbird ended his song. There was no noise, there was no wind and no cars interrupted the silence.

It was as if Andill himself had sealed off the place for the special occasion. They all stood, their eyes fixed on the big rock across the street that was encircled by a spiked iron fence to keep visitors at bay.

Francis led the way. He crossed the road and opened the metal gate in the hedge.

Nick, Milo and Ellie looked at each other.

"Okay, let's go talk to a rock," Nick said evenly. He shrugged and followed Francis with Ellie and Milo following right behind him.

"There's nothing to worry about," Roberta said to Lily and Andrew.

"Are you sure about this?" Andrew asked.

"Absolutely," Roberta said and crossed the road.

"I still can't believe any of this is real," Andrew quietly said to Lily.

Lily gave him a kiss, but didn't smile.

"It's real," she said.

She took her husband by the hand and followed Roberta. Francis still stood by the gate and politely bowed as they entered the field. When he pushed the gate shut and turned, he saw that Corisander was sitting by his feet. Francis kneeled down.

"I wish I knew what you were thinking right now," Francis said.

"Meow," Corisander replied.

If he could, Corisander thought, would he really tell them?

Leaning on his cane, Francis rose and walked to the others. Corisander watched them, standing at a respectful distance from the King Stone.

The three children of the flow, Nick, Milo and Ellie … how their lives had changed, how much they had discovered about themselves and the world around them in the short time since their arrival.

Lily and Andrew, holding hands and standing just behind their young ones … elves and selkies, earth and water. Corisander saw the flow of deep love surround them.

Roberta stood just slightly apart from them. He felt the old woman's heart burst with joy when Lily took her hand, pulling her closer.

Francis stepped up next to them and then he spoke. Corisander didn't need to hear the words. They would be words of speculation and hope and belief.

It didn't matter. What mattered was the presence of the three Archers.

Corisander lay down in the grass, watching the Archers

as they jumped over the iron fence and approached the King Stone.

When they touched it, a gentle ripple ran from the rock, pulsing through the earth and through the air.

The King Stone began to glow and vibrate in the glistening summer sun.

THE END

... FOR NOW

THE CHAMP

At the tender age of one hundred and fifteen, Wilber Patorkin he's the oldest man alive in the United States of America, the champion of age.

His body is failing him gloriously, his legs will barely carry him, his quivering lips and dentures turn his words into meaningless babble... and yet he has the clearest brain and the brightest eyes you'll ever come across. His steps may be tiny, but his story is epic. His words may be few, but his mind goes beyond your wildest imagination.

Join Wilber on a most unlikely journey and be prepared - you just may discover yourself along the way.

What reviewers write: *"Eckhart has created a wonderfully warm and eccentric main character in 115-year-old Wilber Patorkin." – "A story of friendship, mortality, and good vs. evil, it was so good I couldn't put it down." – "A crossover between Amélie Poulain and Benjamin Button." – "The style is a compelling mix between Stephen King & JD Salinger."*

BARNABY SMITH

They always asked Barnaby, "Why do you want to fly?" And he'd always reply, "Why do you want to breathe?"

Barnaby Smith is the tale of a despairing psychiatrist and her patient - a story about life, love, belief, compromise and freedom ... and yes, the dream of human flight. Six months after her son's suicide, psychiatrist Dr. Martha Lewis takes on a position at Brooklyn's St. Joseph's Hospital where she is given the charge of the Barnaby Smith. Barnaby has tried to fly, like a bird, his entire life. He has jumped off roofs nine times, he has broken every bone in his body ... and he has been at St. Joseph's, heavily medicated for his own safety, for the past twenty-three years. Martha makes it her obsession to bring this man back into life, to save him ... only to realize that Barnaby just may be the key to her own salvation.

What reviewers write: *"We should all be so fortunate to find the Barnaby in our lives to guide us forward." – "Don't miss out on this amazing trip through the lives of wonderful people. You will be the richer for the experience." – "Mr. Eckhart reached through the pages and dropped me into another world." – "Barnaby Smith will take you on a mystical journey through continents, during which you'll laugh, cry, love, learn, wonder ... and fly!"*

HOME

When eighty-two-year-old Max Flynn meets Walt Miller, he can't believe his eyes. Walt is not only seven and a half feet tall, he also looks exactly like the giant Max knew as a child during Coney Island's golden years. Max, a former cop who spent his life protecting the island and the people walking upon it, decides to solve the mystery of 'the impossible man'. As Max learns more and more about Walt Miller, he finds friendship, love, a dark secret and a world beyond his wildest dreams.

This is a novel about home, about the earth, about the land we walk on. This is also a novel about being mindful and doing the right thing. In Walt's words: "Max Flynn gives me hope. There must be others like him. People who care deeply, deeply enough to hear the heartbeat of the land they walk on. They are the future. They will be the balance."

What reviewers write: *"The heart truly is where Home is." – "It made me cry and left me feeling new, forever young and hopeful." – "Imaginative, life affirming and magical." – "The perfect recipe for a heartwarming book." – "This just has to be made into a movie."*

Daniel Martin Eckhart is a screenwriter and a novelist. Many moons ago, long before discovering his love for storytelling, he guarded the life of the Pope in the Vatican, worked for the United Nations in Israel, Lebanon, Iraq and Iran and studied acting in New York at the glorious Neighborhood Playhouse School of the Theatre.

These days the author lives on a 17th century farm in Switzerland together with his wife, three children, a monster dog and a psychotic cat.

Printed in Poland
by Amazon Fulfillment
Poland Sp. z o.o., Wrocław